ink and ivy

Sara Martin

ISBN: 978-0-473-43615-5

1

The sky darkened with angry black clouds. Gripping the handlebars tightly, I pedalled onwards. Mum had warned me about the approaching storm, but I hadn't listened. It had been sunny an hour ago. I never imagined the weather would turn so quickly. Now, I was desperate to get home before it inevitably poured down.

The air grew heavier and more oppressive by the minute. I wasn't going to make it. A droplet landed on the back of my exposed neck and rolled down my collar, drawing a shiver. The next thing I knew, I was drenched. The rain pelted down with such force I could barely see where I was going. My bike wobbled as the wind whipped at me.

The streetlights hadn't turned on yet although it was dark. A passing car's headlights provided a temporary reprieve. I powered on through the storm, sodden and shivering. The thought of getting home and changing into warm, dry pyjamas kept me going.

My bike glided along the slick pavement until it struck a pothole. With a jolt, the bike slipped out from beneath me. My leg hit the ground, then my palms came down with a scrape on the pavement. Dirty water splashed up my side. I hurt all over. Teeth gritted, I pulled myself from the gutter. My palms were raw and my leg was going to get an awful bruise, but that seemed to be the extent of my injuries.

The damage to my bike was far worse. It was all twisted out of shape. I put my hand in my skirt pocket to retrieve my cell phone, but my fingers grasped thin air. A sense of dread filled my stomach. I examined the gutter and saw my phone, its back cover and battery lying in the stream of water. I swore and let out a moan of exasperation.

Now what am I going to do? I gathered up the pieces of my phone and put them in the pocket of my backpack, although I knew there was no use in trying to save it.

The rain wasn't letting up. I had to walk—there was no other option. Perhaps I could find shelter somewhere along the way. I walked my mangled bike along the footpath. My body ached and my teeth chattered. Finally, I glimpsed a light up ahead. I quickened my pace.

The light's source was a small strip of shops. I could duck into one and call Mum to pick me up. I peered through the window of the first shop—a bakery. No movement came from within. I tried the door, but it was locked. The next two shops had closed signs on their doors. I was losing hope, but then, I saw a faint light from the next shop window.

No open or closed sign and the door was shut. I clasped the handle and it relinquished. I was so surprised, I almost toppled over. Gathering myself, I took in my surroundings. The vast, grand room was furnished with exquisite antiques and art. Paintings and photographs in ornate frames covered the walls. A grandfather clock struck five. Had I entered a shop or accidentally walked into a wealthy nobleman's living room?

The closer I looked, the more certain I became that it was a shop. Display cabinets housed necklaces, rings, and bracelets. Glass dishes overflowed with beads, brooches, and various trinkets. Beautiful scarves and shawls were folded and boxed, while delicate laces, silks, and linens were neatly shelved.

I marvelled at all the beautiful objects. A gorgeous piano stood in the corner. I couldn't resist taking a closer look. I traversed the layers of rugs and inspected the old instrument. When I pressed a key, it stuck, sending a deep sound reverberating around the room and startling me. Someone cleared their throat behind me.

"Can I help you?" said a deep, velvety voice.

I swung around, startled. A tall, elegant woman stood behind me. She had pitch-black hair down to her waist, and she wore a long, flowy dress. She reminded me of Morticia Addams. Her arms were crossed, and her lips were pursed.

My voice came out in a squeak. "I-I'm sorry. I was just—"

The woman raised a thin eyebrow.

"I was just fascinated. I've never seen a shop like this before. It's wonderful."

The woman softened, a warm smile spreading across her pale face.

I relaxed. She wasn't so scary after all.

She examined me closer. "You're soaking wet. What happened?"

I prayed I hadn't traipsed mud all through the shop. Taking a cursory glance around the room, I was relieved when I didn't see any damage. I tried to explain my situation. "I got caught in the storm on my bike. Then, I fell off it. I'm okay, just a bit wet. And cold. I was walking down the street, looking for somewhere to take shelter from the rain. The door was open, so I just wandered in. I hope you don't mind."

"You're hurt," the woman exclaimed. She took my hand and examined the graze.

"I'm fine." I instinctively snatched my hand back and pulled my sweater sleeves down over my palms. "I need to call my mum and get her to pick me up."

"You're welcome to use the phone."

"Thanks. That would be great."

"But, first, why not use the bathroom to clean yourself up a bit? There's a first-aid kit in the cabinet too. Then, you can call your mum, and I'll make you a cup of tea while you wait."

"Okay, that sounds good. Thanks. Where's the bathroom?"

"Come with me."

I followed the woman through a beaded curtain at the back of the shop, and we emerged in a small corridor with a steep, narrow staircase at the end.

"Mind your head," she said as we ascended. The height of the ceiling barely accommodated climbing the stairs.

We reached a landing with two doorways.

The woman motioned to the left. "Just through there, my dear. There are fresh towels in the hamper. Come back down when you're ready. Take all the time you need."

"Thank you."

The woman returned downstairs.

I nudged open the door. The small bathroom contained a toilet, shower and vanity. Potted plants stood on the windowsill, and vintage Guerlain and Chanel perfume bottles on the vanity. Reaching into the cane hamper, I grabbed a clean towel and flannel. I looked at myself in the mirror. The rain had washed away most of the dirt, but I still looked down-trodden.

I stripped down to my polka-dot undies and blue t-shirt bra to inspect the damage. It wasn't as bad as I'd expected. My

shins were b[illegible] f
me seemed f[illegible] n
dried myself [illegible] I
squeezed ou[illegible] y
clothes were [illegible] y
were cold, an[illegible]

When I l[illegible] g
caught my at[illegible] I
could see int[illegible] g
to take a clos[illegible] l
and a chair. [illegible] a
large drawing [illegible] l
the village. I [illegible] and
I thought better of it.

I went back downstairs. The woman ushered me into the kitchen where a kettle boiled on the stove.

"Feeling better?" she asked.

"Yep. Thank you."

"You look cold. Here—" she removed a grey sweater from the back of a chair "—put this on. My nephew left it here. Sorry if it's not that clean, but at least it's dry."

I gratefully took the sweater, removed my damp school jersey, and put it on. It was huge on me, but so thick and warm. It did smell faintly like boy, though.

"Would you like a cup of tea?" the woman asked.

"Yes, please!" Just the thought of a nice cup of tea warmed me up.

"Coming right up. Oh, by the way, the phone's over there by the door." She pointed it out.

"Thanks." I picked up the phone and called home. It rang several times before someone answered.

"Hello?"

"Hey. It's Ivy. I need a ride home."

"What's happened? Where are you?"

"Well, I went to go return my overdue library books, but I got caught in the storm on the way home."

Mum sighed. "Where are you now?"

"I'm in a shop."

"Where is this shop, then?"

"Uh, hold on." I asked the woman the address and repeated it to Mum. "28 Islington Lane."

"I'll have to look that up. I'll get there as soon as I can."

"Okay."

She hung up.

I sighed. At least the ordeal was over and I'd be safe and warm at home soon. I sat down at the table. The woman placed a tray with a cup of tea and gingernut cookies in front of me.

"Thanks."

"Everything sorted?" the woman asked.

I nodded.

"Good."

I dunked a gingernut in the milky tea. After a few sips, I felt much warmer. The woman joined me at the table. The smell of her perfume comforted me; a mixture of leather, vanilla and tobacco. I decided to bring up something that was on my mind. "When I was upstairs, I noticed a studio…"

"So, you saw Julian's studio."

"It's not yours?"

She shook her head. "Julian is my nephew. He's an artist with a wonderful talent for drawing. He helps me out with the shop, and I let him use the room above."

"Oh. Seems like a good arrangement."

"It is."

I wondered what her nephew was like and how old he might be. There certainly weren't any Julians at my school that I knew of.

"So, tell me a bit about yourself, dear. We haven't introduced ourselves properly."

"Well, my name's Ivy Beckett. I'm seventeen years old, and I'm in my final year at Bridgeway High School."

"Ivy. That's a pretty name." The woman's dark eyes searched me. "Are you an artist too, like my nephew?"

I was taken aback. I shook my head. "No, not me. I'm terrible at art."

"Oh. That's strange."

"How so?"

"It was just a feeling I had, that's all. I can sense you have an artistic spirit."

"Really? I don't think so."

The woman smiled warmly. "You're still young. You're still discovering things about yourself."

Despite the fact this woman didn't even know me, her words mesmerised me. I couldn't help taking them to heart. For some reason, they resonated with me.

"My name's Priscilla, by the way. This is my shop, Opulence. I sell art and various treasures from around the world."

"This is the most beautiful shop I've ever seen. It's weird. I never even knew about this place."

Priscilla laughed. "I wish this shop will always remain a hidden gem."

"But don't you struggle to get customers?"

"I have a small, but loyal clientele. I prefer it this way."

Outside, the rain eased. I had just finished my last mouthful of tea when there was a knock at the door. Priscilla got up to answer it. I knew it was Mum, so I followed her. Priscilla opened the door and Mum swept in.

"There you are. Come on, we're going home." She tugged me away.

"Thank you, Priscilla," I called on my way to the car.

Priscilla smiled and waved from the doorway. "Do visit again." She disappeared back inside the dimly lit shop.

I remembered to grab my bike. "Can we put this in the boot?"

"What happened? It's broken!"

"I had an accident."

"Are you all right?"

"Yeah. I'm fine."

Mum opened the boot and tossed the bike inside.

We climbed in the car and began the drive home.

"Is now a bad time to mention I broke my phone as well?"

Mum didn't answer. She took a deep breath and pressed a little harder on the accelerator.

2

The storm cleared overnight. I woke with my alarm at seven o'clock, the sun streaming in my bedroom window. I stumbled out of bed and got ready for school.

After a quick shower and Nutella on toast for breakfast, I left for school. When I arrived, Lana sat under the oak tree by the school's entrance. She had a folder balanced on her knees and was furiously scribbling away on a pad of paper.

"Hey," I said, tossing my backpack on the ground and sitting down next to her.

Lana didn't look at me.

"You okay?" I asked.

"I need to get this assignment done before third period."

"Your history essay?"

Lana nodded as she continued to write.

"Did you forget it's due today?"

"No. I haven't had the chance to work on it. I've been flat out at the hospital. The other volunteer has been off sick, so I've picked up her shifts."

"You know you can always say no, right? You're a volunteer. They can't make you do anything."

Lana shrugged. "I like working there. Besides, I need to be able to handle this kind of workload. Med school is, like, *insanely* demanding."

"Yeah, I guess. But don't overdo it, okay?"

"I won't."

"Well, I'll leave you to it then." I pulled out a novel to read for the remaining few minutes before form class.

When the bell rang, Lana and I parted ways to go to our separate classes.

"See you in English," I said.

"See ya," Lana said, putting her folder and pencil case away in her bag.

When everyone had arrived and settled in form class, Miss April called the roll and then read the day's notices. "In three weeks' time, the school is having its annual careers fair. All senior students are expected to attend. Your parents will receive letters in the mail about it."

I had attended the careers fair the previous year. It had been a bunch of stalls set up by reps from different universities and trade schools. I wasn't looking forward to going, but I was sure Mum would be eager to attend. It wouldn't make any difference, anyway. The decision had already been made for me. The law programme at Hill University was considered the best in the country.

When Miss April finished reading the notices, we chatted among ourselves until the bell rang for first period. I made my way to English, joining the other students flowing into the classroom. I sat down at my desk. Lana arrived shortly after and sat beside me.

"Did you finish your history assignment?" I asked.

"Not yet, but I can work on it at interval. I'll get it done. Don't worry."

"I'm not worried." I knew Lana would never turn in an unfinished assignment. She was the top student in the school. She would never risk a hit to her GPA. It would put her scholarship hopes in jeopardy.

Our English teacher, Mr. Donaldson, arrived in class. He looked dishevelled as usual, unshaven and glasses askew. "Books out everyone," he said as he went to his desk.

After a few minutes of reading, Mr. Donaldson got up and came around, placing sheets of paper on everyone's desk. When he got to me, I picked up the piece of paper. It was a creative writing assignment. The topic was *an accident*. My brain was already at work trying to think of an idea.

Mr. Donaldson stood at the whiteboard and, with a green marker, wrote *An Accident - 800 words. Due Wednesday 21 March*. He cleared his throat. "Attention, everyone."

There was a rustle as everyone put their books away.

"It's that time of year again. The creative writing assignment counts for five literacy credits. Your story must include a reference to an accident—literal or otherwise. The interpretation is up to you."

"Sir?" a voice asked from the back of the class.

"Yes, Jamie?"

"Are there any restrictions on what we can write?"

"Anything goes, but please keep it PG. No explicit sex scenes. No gratuitous violence."

"Boring," Jamie grumbled.

Laughter rippled through the room.

We spent the rest of class reading short stories for inspiration and brainstorming ideas. I loved writing, so I knew I would have a lot of fun with this assignment. When I left for my next class, economics, I was still thinking about what to write. I could barely concentrate while Mr. Elliot droned on about supply and demand curves.

Lana spent morning interval holed up in the library, getting her essay done, so I didn't see her again until lunch time.

"Did you manage to hand your essay in on time?" I asked, approaching the bench behind C block, where she sat eating her lunch.

"Of course."

"Phew!"

"Yeah. It was really down to the last minute."

"Have you thought about what you're gonna write about for the creative writing assignment?" I asked, sitting down and taking out my lunch box.

"No. I kinda suck at writing."

"What are you saying? You're a great writer."

"You're much better than me. Anyway, what about you? Do you know what you're going to write?"

"I have a few ideas."

"That's good. If you end up with a spare idea, chuck it my way. I'm useless at story ideas."

"Sure, if you really need it."

"Oh, I will." Lana got up and tossed her apple core in the bin. Upon her return, her eyes fell to my hands. "Oh my God! What happened to your hand?"

I pulled my sleeves down. "It's nothing."

"Doesn't look like nothing."

I reluctantly showed her my palms.

"What happened?"

"I fell off my bike yesterday."

"Ouch."

"I'm okay. The bike isn't in such great shape, though. My

phone got destroyed too. So, don't bother texting me."

"That sucks."

"Yeah." I sighed. "But at least something good came out of it."

"What do you mean?"

"Have you heard of Opulence? It's this amazing shop, just outside of town. There's an artist's studio there too."

"I think I've heard of it. I think my mum has mentioned it before."

"It's like something out of a dream. I met this strange, kind of mystical woman there. I can't stop thinking about something she said."

"What did she say?"

"Well, I can't remember exactly what she said, but it was like she knew things about me. Things I don't even know about myself."

"Is she psychic or something? Did she have a crystal ball?"

I chuckled. "Well, she seemed like the type of woman who would have a crystal ball."

"Are you going to go back there?"

"Yeah. Probably should. I borrowed a sweater and I need to return it. Long story."

"Well, let me know if you go back. I want to know more about this woman. She sounds interesting."

I nodded. "I'll go back tomorrow."

The next day, I hopped on the bus after school. I got off at the nearest stop to Islington Lane. The sweater was stowed in my backpack. I headed towards the clock tower and found myself on that lane of pretty houses and cute shops once again.

I glanced around, but I couldn't find Opulence anywhere. For a moment, I wondered if I were crazy. Had the encounter with Opulence and Priscilla really happened? It felt like it was just a dream. I cast the thought aside. I was being silly. The fact I had the sweater in my bag was evidence enough that it had really occurred. I finally spied the entry, slightly recessed—farther back from the other shops. Opulence was delicately carved into a wooden sign above the door.

Once again, the door was closed. I tugged the handle, but this time, it was locked tight. *That's odd. It was open later than this on the day of the storm.* I pressed my face against the glass and peered through the lace curtain. All was still.

"Hello?" A male voice came from behind me, throwing me off-guard.

I straightened and turned. A young man with dark, wavy hair stood there. He was green-eyed and fair, almost elfin looking. A hint of recognition tugged at my mind but I wasn't sure from where. He looked at me with a searching gaze, and I felt utterly exposed. "I, uh… I was looking for Priscilla."

The man smiled, dimples forming in his cheeks. "Ah. The shop's closed right now, but she might be in later. She sort of keeps her own hours. You never know when the shop is going to be open or closed. Regular customers know it's best to call to make an appointment." The man produced a key from his pocket and unlocked the door. "You wanna wait inside?"

"Yes, please." I followed him in.

I was no less in awe of the shop than the first time I had seen it. This time, I studied the room more closely. My eyes opened to more wonderful treasures, like the display of lacquered boxes and a collection of Japanese cast-iron teapots.

"Can I get you something? Water? Tea?" the man asked. He was just as accommodating as Priscilla.

"No, thanks." I realised this man might be Priscilla's nephew and, if that were the case, there would be little point in waiting around. "Are you Julian?"

The man looked perplexed. "Yes, I am. How did you know?"

"I think I have something of yours." I shimmied off my backpack and pulled out the grey raglan sweater.

"That looks familiar. Thank you." He took the sweater. "Why did you have this?"

"It's a long story. The short version is Priscilla lent it to me."

Julian removed his jacket, revealing a tightly fitting white t-shirt. He put the sweater on.

I briefly wondered whether I should have washed it first, and I prayed it didn't smell.

"Are you the girl who turned up here a few days ago, soaking wet and shivering?"

"Yeah. That was me." I felt my cheeks redden. How did he know about that?

Julian chuckled. "Priscilla told me all about it. Thanks for bringing my sweater back. I've actually been wondering where it was."

"That's okay. It was the least I could do after Priscilla helped me out."

"Well, thanks. I appreciate it."

He smiled dreamily, making my heart flutter.

His eyes searched my face. "Hey, do I know you from somewhere?"

So, it wasn't just me, then. He felt it too.

"Yeah, I think I've seen you before."

Julian paused for a moment, thinking. "I know. I've seen you at Lucky Books."

"Oh, really? I guess I go there quite often." Lucky Books was a second-hand bookstore in town. With my addiction to books, it was one of my top shops to visit when I went to town.

"I work there."

"That explains it, then."

"Yeah."

"Maybe I'll see you the next time I go there."

"You probably will. Come and say hi."

"Sure." I was glad the sweater was back with its owner, but I didn't want to leave just yet. "Do you mind if I look around for a while?"

"Of course not. Take your time. I'll be upstairs. Just close the door behind you when you leave."

"Okay."

Julian disappeared down the corridor. His footsteps echoed as he climbed the stairs. He must be going to his studio to work.

I looked around the shop until my curiosity was finally quenched. Priscilla didn't return while I was there, but somehow, I felt sure I would see her again.

When I got home, the smell of dinner cooking flooded my nostrils.

"Ivy," Dad called from the lounge.

He must have heard me come in. I turned into the lounge, threw my backpack on the floor and collapsed into an armchair. Dad was on the couch, a beer in his hand. His tie was loose around his neck.

"Hey, Dad. How was your day?"

"It was a tough day. Two people lost their jobs."

"Really?"

"Yeah."

"But you're fine, right?"

Dad nodded. "I'd be the last person to lose my job. How would the newspaper make any money without me?"

I gave a small sigh of relief. "You scared me there."

"Don't you worry about me." Dad chuckled. "I got you something."

"What is it?"

He got up and pressed a smooth, rectangular object into my hand. A new cell phone!

"I had it set up so it has your old number."

I turned the phone in my hand, its shiny screen beneath my fingertips. "Thanks, Dad! I love it."

Mum had told me not to expect a new phone after I broke the last one.

"I don't like not being able to contact you when you're out."

I gave him a big hug.

"There's something else to tell you too," he said when I broke away.

"Oh?"

Mum's footsteps came down the hallway. She peered into the room.

"Dinner's ready."

"Coming," Dad said, about to leave the room.

"Wait. What were you going to tell me?"

"Never mind. I think your Mum has something planned."

Before I could question him any further, he was off down the hallway.

3

I had tried to make a start on my creative writing assignment several times over the past few days. Every time I started, something blocked me from getting past the first few sentences.

I sat at my computer, determined to get something down this time. Anything. The cursor blinked tauntingly on the blank Word document.

Okay, Ivy. Just write.

I poised my fingers on the keyboard. With a deep breath and a clear head, I let a torrent of words flow out.

It was the dead of night. A chill wind picked up. I stood facing the other side of the road. He was there, waiting for me as he said he would be. I was so happy. I walked out onto the road. His arms beckoned to me. I saw the headlights first. Two bright beams. They blinded me. The car screeched and swerved, but my legs were concrete.

"Ivy?"

The car hit me, ripping a gurgling scream from my insides.

"Ivy?"

Everything went black after that.

"Ivy? Can I come in?" Mum opened the door a crack.

I sighed and closed the document. My flow had been destroyed. "Yes?"

Mum wore a dress and heels and was fully made up.

"You look nice. Going somewhere?"

"Yes, and so are you. We're going out to dinner. You should get ready soon."

"Oh?" I was a little perplexed. We rarely went out for dinner, especially not on a school night. "What's the occasion?"

"You'll have to wait and see." Mum had a glimmer in her eye. "We're booked for seven o'clock, so we'll leave just before then. Get changed out of your uniform. Wear something nice." She left before I could ask her to elaborate.

I racked my brain, trying to think about what was so special about tonight, but nothing surfaced. By all appearances, it was just a regular Wednesday night. I wondered if this had anything to do with what Dad had mentioned the other day. He hadn't brought it up again since then. I supposed I would find out soon enough.

After a quick browse through my wardrobe, I chose a long skirt paired with a silk tank top. I put on a dab of lipstick and some mascara. A spritz of Marc Jacobs's Daisy was the final touch.

"We're leaving!" Mum yelled.

I grabbed my wallet and my phone from the outer pocket

of my school bag and transferred them into a clutch. Before heading out the door, I gave myself a quick once-over in the floor-length mirror. Upon determining I looked fine, I left and met my parents at the car. Dad wore the tie with turtles on it that I had given him when I was a kid.

Fifteen minutes later, we arrived at my favourite restaurant —La Bella Rossa—an upmarket Italian place on the waterfront. I wondered if they chose this restaurant because the special occasion had something to do with me. I was overflowing with curiosity now.

A waiter greeted us when we entered and took us to our table. It was busy for a Wednesday night. Couples out on dates and groups of friends chatted and laughed over their meals while jazz music played.

Dad ordered wine for the table. The waiter poured us each a glass. I was bursting to ask my parents what this was all about.

"So, what is it, then? Can you tell me now? Pretty please?"

Dad glanced sideways at Mum, and she gave a small nod. He took a sip of his wine and then began. "We've been keeping a secret from you."

"A secret? What secret?" I would have been concerned if it weren't for the proud looks on my parents' faces.

"Ever since you were born, we've been putting money aside for you. A little bit each week."

My mouth gaped in surprise. I had no idea my parents had been doing that for me.

"Really? So, what's the money for?"

Mum looked at me as if it were obvious. "It's for your education, honey."

I had always assumed the burden of paying for my education would fall entirely upon myself, so I was thrilled by this development.

"We wanted to celebrate because the account is now fully funded," Dad explained.

"What does that mean?"

"It means everything is sorted. There's enough in there to cover all your university costs, course fees, accommodation, food, textbooks. You can graduate debt-free."

It took a while for me to process what this meant, but when it finally sank in, I was over the moon. No obligatory crappy part-time job. No eating two-minute noodles to survive. I could have a worry-free university lifestyle and devote myself entirely to my studies.

"This is incredible! Thank you. I can't believe it." My head spun. The wine didn't help.

"Now, don't go getting too excited," Mum said, suddenly sombre. "It's a lot of money. More than we have in our own savings account. By giving you this money, we expect you to use it responsibly."

I was a little taken aback. I had always been responsible with money. How could they possibly think otherwise?

"I know that. Of course, I will."

Mum looked at Dad and then turned back to me. "We just have one condition."

"Oh, really? What's that?" I asked with a hint of trepidation.

"We think it's best you study something practical. Something likely to lead to a job."

"Oh. I guess that's fair." I didn't consider it an unreasonable demand, but it did somewhat put a damper on things.

"It's tough out there these days. The financial crisis, unemployment…"

"I know."

"You need a career in mind. A sensible career."

I turned to Dad. He had an arts degree himself, perhaps he thought differently on the subject.

"Your mum's right, Ivy. It's not like it was back when I was your age. Not just any degree will do."

It's not like I had been considering an arts degree, anyway. When I was nine years old, I told my parents I wanted to be a lawyer when I grew up. I could still remember the proud looks on their faces. Ever since then, they have encouraged me on that path—Mum especially.

She worked as a PA to Natalie Turner—an accomplished, successful female lawyer. To Mum, Natalie Turner was the epitome of success, and she seemed to fancy the idea I would become just like her. She was already trying to line me up for work experience at the law firm over the holidays.

"I'm going to study law," I said, reminding them.

A look of relief swept Mum's face. "Good. We all agree. You will go to law school."

I nodded, doing my best to look enthusiastic about the idea.

Next year, I would start the degree that would set me on the path to become a lawyer. It was strange because I just couldn't seem to picture myself as an attorney. I shrugged the feeling away.

This is what I want, isn't it?

4

Over the next few days, I found myself on a roll with my creative writing assignment. I finished it several days before it was due. I believed it was the best thing I had ever written. On Wednesday morning, I printed it and popped it in my schoolbag, ready to turn in.

When I arrived at school, I couldn't find Lana at any of our usual spots. *Is she sick?* I brushed the thought aside. Lana would have to be at death's door before she took a day off from school. Maybe she was just running late. Although, that was also unlike her.

Lana still hadn't shown up by the time I had to leave for form class. While Miss April read the notices, I held my phone under my desk and discreetly sent Lana a text message.

Didn't see you this morning. Are you at school today?

I slipped my phone back into the pocket of my plaid skirt.

On my way to first period, I checked my phone. *No new messages. Oh, well.* I'd find out whether she was there or not in second period English.

I kept my eyes open for her on the way to English. When I

arrived, Lana's desk was still empty and remained so as the rest of the students filtered in. We were supposed to read in silence for the first ten minutes of class, but everyone chatted since Mr. Donaldson hadn't shown up yet.

The door swung open. Everyone quietened, thinking it was him, but it was Lana. She didn't look particularly tired or sick, yet there was something off about her. She looked somewhat bedraggled, with strands of her black hair falling out of her ponytail and her blouse half-untucked. Normally, her appearance was no less than immaculate.

She dumped her backpack down and sat beside me.

"You're here," I said, relieved.

"I was just a little late. That's all. Slept over the top of my alarm."

"I texted you."

"Sorry. I was in such a hurry this morning, I left my phone at home."

"Well, I'm glad you're here."

Mr. Donaldson arrived to class, and everyone got their books out.

"Late night at the hospital again?" I whispered to Lana from behind my paperback.

She nodded.

After a few minutes of reading, Mr. Donaldson got up and came around, collecting the assignments. Anxious chatter swelled. When he got to me, I happily handed mine over. Lana didn't look so confident. Mr. Donaldson had to pry the assignment from her hand. As it left her tight grip, she slumped and let out a small sigh of defeat.

"What are you so worried about? You always get excellence," I reminded her. I couldn't remember a time when she got anything less than top marks.

"Thanks, but I'm not so sure this time. I really left this to the last minute. I was up all night finishing it."

"Again? I thought you learnt your lesson after the history essay."

"What lesson? I work better under pressure."

By lunch time, Lana seemed to have recovered from her state of exhaustion. The colour had returned to her face, and her eyes had regained their usual brightness.

"I don't know how you do it," I mused.

"Do what?"

"How you work your butt off at the hospital, piano lessons and the debate team, and you still ace every assignment."

"Well, it's not easy." Lana sighed, tucking her hair behind her ear.

"Are you working tonight?"

"No. I have the night off."

"Good. Let's do something. Come to my house and we can watch a movie or something. You need to stop working so hard for a moment."

"I wish I could. My parents are having relatives over for dinner and I have to be there."

"Oh. Some other time, then?"

Lana nodded. "Can't wait."

A week flew by. Lana always had an excuse not to hang out after school or on the weekend. She was either working at the hospital, studying or busy with one of her many extra-curricular activities. I could tell she was burning out, and she really needed time to chill. Her parents were very strict with her. My parents were harsh, but hers were something else.

Lana wasn't working on Saturday afternoon, so I took matters into my own hands. I arrived on her doorstep with a ton of DVDs and plenty of junk food for sustenance. Knocking on the door, I prayed I wouldn't be turned away.

The door creaked open. Lana's mother, Mrs. Wu, peered out. She was a squat woman, with bluntly cropped hair and beady eyes. If she were surprised to see me, her expression didn't betray it.

"Hello, Ivy. Are you here to see Lana?"

"Yes, Mrs. Wu. May I come in?" I asked in the politest voice I could muster.

Mrs. Wu looked incredulous, but she stepped aside and let me in.

I walked down the hallway of the Wu family's modest home. I climbed the stairs and knocked on Lana's bedroom door. Silence. I tried one more time before pushing the door open.

Lana was at her desk, hunched over a biology textbook, a pair of headphones atop her head. I walked up to her and yanked her headphones off. She jumped in fright.

"Geez Ivy," she said, catching her breath. "You scared the bejeebus out of me. What are you doing here?"

"Remember, you promised we'd hang out?"

"I know. I've been busy."

"You need to stop being busy for a minute and relax. You've been so tense lately. Not to mention your social life has gone out the window."

"Social life? What social life?"

"My point exactly."

Lana sighed. "Well, you're here now. I guess studying for my biology test can wait until tomorrow."

"That's the spirit."

Lana eyed the bags I carried. "What did you bring?"

I rifled through the selection. "*The Shining, Annie Hall, The Princess Bride, Spirited Away*..."

"Good stuff."

"And I brought chocolate, chips and coke."

"The three C's."

"Shall we go downstairs?"

"I'll have to kick Bing and Jack out of the lounge."

"Is that okay?"

"It's fine. They're not supposed to be watching TV, anyway."

We went downstairs to the lounge which was dominated by bookcases. The TV set was small and unassuming. Bing and Jack were watching Cartoon Network.

"Out, you two. We're going to watch a movie."

"Why? Do we have to?" Jack asked, frowning.

"Yes. You've been watching TV all day."

Bing and Jack groaned.

"Out. Or I'll go get Mum."

Their eyes widened with fear and they quickly left. Now, we had the room to ourselves.

"What movie do you wanna watch?" I asked.

"Something we can talk through and it won't matter."

"*The Princess Bride*?" We already knew it by heart.

"Perfect."

Lana set up the DVD player and inserted the disk. I made myself comfortable on the couch and opened a bag of chips. Lana joined me momentarily.

"Sorry I haven't been hanging out with you a lot lately," she said.

"It's all good. I know you've been busy."

"The hospital has sort of become my life now."

"As long as you're happy."

Lana nodded. "I'm more certain than ever that I want to be a doctor."

"It's good you're so sure," I said, lamenting my own uncertainty.

"What about you? Do you still want to be a lawyer?"

"Yeah, I guess. My parents told me they're going to pay to put me through uni, so it's pretty much set in stone now, anyway. They're not going to let me change my mind all of a sudden."

"Wow. That's big news. How come you didn't tell me?"

I shrugged. "I guess I didn't want to rub it in or anything. Med School is expensive, and I know it's going to be tough for you."

"I don't mind. That's what scholarships are for." Lana reached for a handful of chips. "You've been holding out on me. What else haven't you told me? Did you end up going back to Opulence?"

"Yeah."

"And did the psychic lady have any more words of wisdom for you?"

"She wasn't there."

Lana examined me through narrowed eyes. She must have sensed there was something I wasn't telling her.

"So, what happened, then?"

"A guy let me into the shop."

"A guy, eh? Was he cute?"

"Well…"

A grin spread across Lana's face. "He was, wasn't he?"

I sighed. "Yes. He was cute."

Lana squealed with delight. "I knew it! Tell me more."

"There's not much to tell. He's Priscilla's nephew. He's tall and dark haired. He's an artist. He works at Lucky Books."

"Now, we have to go to Lucky Books."

"No, we don't."

"Yes, we do! We have to scope him out."

"There will be no scoping."

Lana crossed her arms and pouted "You're such a drag."

I heaved a sigh. "Maybe. We'll see."

"Really?"

"Shhhh. I like this part." I turned up the volume.

5

"Come on. Let's get going," Mum called from the hallway.

What the rush was, I didn't know. I grabbed my purse and my leather jacket before leaving my room. We went straight out the door and to the car.

"I don't know why they make us go to this. It's the same thing every year," I muttered.

"Don't be silly. The more information we can get, the better."

The careers fair always bored me to tears. I would have much rather stayed home and read my book than be dragged around the school hall all evening.

We arrived just after half-past six. The Year 13 Deans stood in the foyer, handing out fabric tote bags emblazoned with the Study Link logo. Tables were set up around the room. As expected, most of the stalls were universities, but the military and police had a presence too. Students and parents swarmed around the stalls of the most popular universities.

Mum yanked me into the crowd around the Hill University stall. After a small battle, we emerged at the front.

"Excuse me," Mum talked over some of the less assertive parents, gaining the attention of one of the reps. "My daughter here wishes to study law next year."

The rep smiled and nodded. "Hill University is the ideal place to study law. We're situated in the heart of the capital, close to parliament and the supreme court."

"Yes, I'm well aware of that." Mum wasn't willing to waste any time. "Can we get a prospectus?"

The rep ducked under the table and took his time retrieving various documents from boxes. Meanwhile, my eyes wandered to different stalls around the room. The Creative Design School, Elias Institute, Linden College of Arts. These were all schools I hadn't even heard of. It made me realise there must be so many different study options out there.

Options I'll never get to explore.

When the rep emerged, he handed over a law degree booklet, an application form and information about student accommodation.

"Thanks," I murmured, stowing the documents in my tote bag.

"Oh, and I should mention there will be an open day at the Law School next month. All serious applicants should attend. All the info is on our website."

"Thank you," Mum said. "That's good to know."

We spent time browsing the other stalls, but only for the other universities with law programmes. It only made Mum even more convinced that Hill University was the best.

I endured the rest of the evening with gritted teeth. When we got home, Mum took the pile of course prospectuses and brochures into the lounge and went through them methodically, from cover to cover. I didn't even get the chance to have a look.

When she was finally done, she turned them over to me. I took them to my room to read through them in bed but found I had lost interest. My mind wandered. I thought about Julian. Since my conversation with Lana, I found he invaded my thoughts more and more often. I wondered if I would see him again.

Maybe Lana was right? I knew where his studio was and where he worked. It wouldn't be that difficult to find him again. As quickly as it had occurred to me, I brushed the thought aside.

On Thursday morning, Mr. Donaldson entered the classroom bearing a stack of papers. I knew they were our assignments—marked and ready to be handed back. It felt like ages since I had handed it in, but it had actually only been a couple of weeks. I trembled in anticipation. Next to me, Lana shifted nervously in her seat, but I knew she did fine.

"Books out," Mr. Donaldson said as he seated himself and placed the stack of papers on his desk.

I couldn't concentrate as I tried to read my book. My stomach swam with nerves. So much effort had gone into that story, and I truly believed I had written something great. It would destroy me if Mr. Donaldson felt differently.

He got up and dished out the marked assignments, placing them silently on each student's desk. He took his time, ambling around the room. Naturally, I was last to receive mine. As soon as it landed on my desk, I flipped to the last page. There, in red ink was a large *E* for *Achieved with Excellence,* the best possible mark. Next to the E, Mr. Donaldson had scrawled *Superb*. I immediately relaxed, all the nervous tension draining out of me. My effort had paid off. I felt validated.

Incredibly, Lana wasn't smiling. Could it be possible? Could she have, for the first time, achieved anything less than excellence? After we had finished reading, Lana showed me her mark. An *M* for *Achieved with Merit*.

"It's still a good mark," I said.

Lana didn't respond. She appeared to be in a state of shock.

"You okay?"

Lana exhaled. "I'm just annoyed with myself."

"One M isn't the end of the world."

"Tell that to my parents."

"You'll make up for it."

Lana nodded. "It's not going to happen again."

"I'm sure it won't."

"So, what did you get?"

Before I could react, she snatched my assignment from me. "Wow. You aced it."

I blushed, suddenly embarrassed.

"Not so surprising, really. Didn't I say you were a much better writer than me?"

"Yeah. But it's still hard to believe."

Lana pushed me. "You're too hard on yourself."

"You can talk."

We burst into laughter.

When the bell rang at the end of class, I put my things away and tossed my backpack over my shoulder. I was halfway out the door when Mr. Donaldson called me.

"Ivy, if you have a minute, could I speak with you?"

I told Lana I'd catch up with her later and then walked over to Mr. Donaldson's desk. Half-drunk cups of tea and screwed up bits of paper were strewn across its surface.

"I trust you're pleased with the mark I gave you?" He squinted at me through his wire-framed glasses.

"Yes, absolutely."

"I wanted to tell you how wonderful your piece was. Riveting stuff. Possibly the best thing I've read all term."

"Really?" I could feel myself blushing. Now this, I hadn't expected.

"Yes. I was most impressed."

"Thank you, sir," I spluttered. For a moment, I thought that was all he had to tell me, but then he cleared his throat and continued.

"Listen, I'm part of a small group of local writers. We send out a monthly newsletter with a few short stories, poems, book recommendations and that kind of thing."

I wondered where he was going with this.

"Would you possibly be so kind as to let me feature your story in next month's newsletter? No pressure. You don't have to if you don't want to."

I bit my lip. As much as I was proud of my writing, the thought of having it circulated made my stomach turn. All that attention would make me feel horribly exposed.

Mr. Donaldson picked up on my reluctance. "You need not give me an answer now. Just think about it and get back to me."

"No, I have my answer," I said. I felt like, if I didn't take the opportunity now, he might never bring it up again. It took a surge of courage, but I agreed to his offer.

"Thank you, Ivy. You won't regret this one bit."

I nodded. I was about to leave when he spoke up again.

"Oh, Ivy?"

"Yes."

"Keep up with your writing. You have talent."

"Thank you, Mr. Donaldson. I will."

"What was that all about?" Lana asked me when I joined her at lunch.

I didn't want to tell her. Especially after the Merit incident. She could get competitive about things like this. But I didn't want to lie to her either. I shrugged and made it out to be no big deal.

"Mr. Donaldson liked my story and wants to send it to some of his friends."

Lana stopped mid-bite into her sandwich. "Wow, Ivy. That's some praise. Mr. Donaldson has had a novel published, hasn't he? I'm sure he knows his stuff."

"Has he? I didn't know that." Mr. Donaldson was a keen writer, but I had no idea he had a book out.

"He's quite private about it, but I'm sure he's mentioned it before."

"Interesting. I wonder what his book is about?"

"No idea. I don't even know what it's called."

"Hey, I know. Why don't we ask Anna? She's sure to know more about it."

Anna was the school librarian. I'd known her since my first day at Bridgeway High School, and we had become good friends since. She knew everything there was to know about books.

"Good idea. Shall we go there now?"

I nodded. We took our bags and traversed the school grounds. The library stood alone—the vast carpark separating it from the rest of the school. Old book smell wafted up my nose as we entered the small room with overstuffed shelves.

Anna wasn't at the desk, so I poked my head around the door into her office. There she stood, bent over a large box full of books.

"Need some help there?" I asked.

"Ivy, is that you?" Anna asked, heaving herself back up.

"You shouldn't be bending over like that," Lana said.

Anna sat down. "You're right. I didn't realise quite how physically demanding this job was until having to do it while pregnant." She smiled wearily.

Lana and I unpacked the box and loaded the books onto a trolley.

"Thanks, girls. I appreciate it."

"Hey, Anna. We wanted to ask you something," Lana said.

"Fire away."

"Do you know anything about Mr. Donaldson's book?"

Anna raised an eyebrow. "So, you know about that, huh?"

We nodded in unison.

"So, what exactly do you want to know?"

"Have you read it?" I asked. "What's it about?"

Anna shook her head. "No, I haven't read it, but I want to. It had a quiet release, and I didn't hear about it until it was already too late. The book is long out of print. The library's copy is lost. I even asked Alfred if he had a spare copy, but he only has his personal copy left which he won't lend. Understandable, of course. Anyway, the book has become something of a rarity."

"That's a shame. I would've liked to read it."

"What brought his book to your attention, anyway?"

"Oh, I was just curious."

"He has taken an interest in Ivy's writing," Lana explained. "He's going to send her story to his writer friends."

"Hmmm. I wonder…" Anna began.

"You wonder what?"

"I wonder where your story might end up. I believe Alfred is well connected in the literary scene."

"Really?"

Anna nodded. "He keeps to himself about it, of course. Anyway, girls, that was the bell. You'd better get going."

On our way back to class, Lana nudged me. "Just imagine. Your story might get read by a literary agent or something."

I hit her on the arm. "Stop it. Don't put ideas like that in my head."

I knew I was being fanciful, but the vague prospect someone important might read my story thrilled me. I couldn't stop daydreaming about it the rest of the day.

That night, over the dinner table, I gleefully announced my E grade to my parents.

"That's wonderful, honey," Dad said, his mouth half-full of roast potato. "I'm so proud of you."

"Well done. Your hard work this year is paying off," Mum said.

"But that's not all," I continued. "Mr. Donaldson liked my story so much he's going to feature it in his newsletter. All the local writers will see it."

"Oh, how nice," Mum said, clearly ignorant to the gravity of the situation.

"He's had a book published, you know. He's a respected author." Actually, I had no idea whether he was respected or not, but it seemed like he would be.

Dad raised his eyebrows. "What's his book called? Do I know it?"

"Uh…I'm not sure. But I'll find out."

"Donaldson?" Mum furrowed her brow. "Can't say I recall

him. Anyway, that's very good of him to be so supportive of his student's work."

"I think it's brilliant," Dad said.

"If his name is respected, maybe you could ask him to be a reference when you apply to university?" Mum suggested.

"Well, I don't see why not…" It hadn't been the first thought to occur to me, but it was a good idea, nonetheless. He would definitely give me a good reference.

After dinner, I received a text message from Lana. *I think I know where we could find Mr. Donaldson's book.*

I fired off a response. *Really? Where?*

My phone buzzed with Lana's reply. *Lucky Books*

She had me there. I supposed it could be worth a try.

6

On Saturday, I drove into town to visit Lucky Books. As much as Lana had wished to accompany me, she was tied up with work once again. It was just as well. If Julian happened to be there, I wouldn't be able to count on her for any semblance of subtlety.

The store was nestled in a covered arcade, along with clothing boutiques, a toy store and a chocolate shop. I reminded myself Julian probably wouldn't even be there. I had no idea what times he worked.

I took a deep breath before pulling open the door to Lucky Books. It was a beautiful, yet crammed shop with floor to ceiling shelves on every wall. A spiral staircase led up to a second floor, where there were yet more books to browse and a small reading area. I scanned the room for signs of Julian. I didn't see him.

Somehow, I felt both relieved and a little disappointed. Okay, more than a little disappointed. I had to remind myself of the reason I was there—Mr. Donaldson's book. It would've helped if I knew the title. The sheer volume of books overwhelmed me. I wasn't sure where to begin my search and stood there cluelessly.

"Need some help?"

I knew that voice. It made the hairs on the back of my neck prick. I turned around. There he was, looking at me with intense green eyes. My heart pounded in my chest.

"Julian," I spluttered.

He smiled, dimples in his cheeks, and I practically melted.

"I was wondering when I'd see you here again," he said.

"Well, here I am."

"Looking for anything in particular?"

"Yeah, I am actually. Do you have a book by Alfred Donaldson?"

"Do you mean the local author?"

"That's right. He's my English teacher."

"Oh, yeah. You go to Bridgeway High, don't you?"

"Uh huh."

"I don't think we have that book, but I'll check our database, though, just in case." Julian went to the counter and typed away on a clunky old desktop computer.

While I stood and waited, I noticed a bunch of flyers on the counter. They were also taped up and displayed around the store. The flyer had a photograph of an art gallery, overlaid with text.

Neighbourhood Story

Five local artists' work on display at Nicholas Gallery

June-July

"Sorry, Ivy. No luck," Julian said, pulling my attention back.

"Oh. That sucks. I really hoped I'd find it here."

"Hmmm…" Julian bit his lip. "I wonder if Priscilla has this book? She's Alfred's friend. If she has it, I'm sure she'd let you borrow it."

"Really? That would be great."

Julian produced a pen and a piece of paper, which he passed across the counter. "Here. Write down your number. I'll contact you if Priscilla has the book."

I wrote down my number and handed the paper back to him. "Thanks, Julian."

"It's no problem." He put the slip in his pocket.

"I'm going to have a look around for a bit."

"Okay. Let me know if you need anything else. I'll be right here."

"Thanks."

My eyes scanned the shelves as I slowly circulated the shop. Every time I visited a bookstore, I could never leave empty handed. A bad habit that I had no intention of breaking. Fortunately, the books here were so cheap. After a thorough browse, I chose a battered copy of *A Room of One's Own*. I took it to the counter, wondering if Julian would make any judgements on me due to my reading taste.

"This one please." I placed the book on the counter.

"That'll be six dollars."

I handed over a five-dollar note and two fifty-cent coins.

While Julian served me, my attention wandered to the art exhibition flyer again.

"A few of my pieces will be on display for that exhibition. If you have time, you should come along."

"Oh, cool. Maybe I will." I took a flyer and stored it in my bag.

"Julian!" A shrill voice erupted from behind me.

A tall girl waltzed in. She had strawberry-blonde hair pulled back in a high ponytail. Black liner rimmed her eyes with a cat-eye flick.

Julian turned his attention to her. "Charlotte. What's the matter?" There was a hint of annoyance in his voice.

"It's two o'clock."

"So?"

"So, you said you'd take me out when you finished your shift!"

"I can't leave straight away. I need to finish up here."

Charlotte groaned. "All right. But hurry up."

"Sorry," Julian returned his attention to me. He handed me my book in a brown paper bag. "Enjoy."

"Thank you."

"I'll be in touch about the book."

The girl, Charlotte, eyed me as I left.

I wondered if she were Julian's girlfriend. My good mood turned down a notch. At least one good thing had emerged from this. Julian had my number.

I stopped off at the chocolate shop before going home. I bought a few pieces of my favourite fudge. After that small indulgence, I felt much happier.

For the rest of the day, I was glued to my phone, constantly checking to see if an unknown number popped up on the screen. I was lying on my bed when my phone finally buzzed. A message from Lana.

Was he there?

I texted, *Yes*

Lana came back immediately. *And?*

I rolled over onto my back, holding the phone above me. *They didn't have the book. Julian is going to contact me if Priscilla has a copy I can borrow.*

So, he has your number?

I could sense the hopefulness in her message.

I replied. *Yes :)*

On Sunday night, I was in full chill-out mode, listening to music in my room and flipping through a magazine. I didn't hear my phone go off, but I saw the screen flash. I immediately paused my iPod and checked my phone. One new message from an unknown number. My heart skipped.

Hey, Ivy. It's Julian. Priscilla has the book and you're allowed to borrow it.

I was in luck. So, I'd get to read Mr. Donaldson's book after all. I replied to Julian's message and saved his number into my contacts.

When I arrived at Opulence the next afternoon, I wondered whether Julian would be around. Priscilla was with a customer, discussing the history of an antique dressing table. I looked around the shop while I waited for her. Eventually, the customer left and Priscilla came to me at once. Dressed in a long slinky black dress, and her lips painted a deep red, she looked as witchy as ever.

"Ivy, my dear. So nice to see you again."

"Thanks. It's good to see you too."

"Have you recovered from your accident?"

I ran my thumb over the scab on my wrist. "Yup. Well, slowly getting there at least."

"That's good. You're here to pick up Alfred's book?"

I nodded. "Thanks for letting me borrow it."

"Quite all right. Alfred is a dear friend. It's wonderful you're showing an interest in his work. Now, where did I put the book?" Priscilla's eyes searched the room. "Ah. I think it's in my bag. I'll go get it." She crossed the shop floor and went behind the beaded curtain. A few seconds later, she reappeared with the book and presented it to me.

I scanned the cover. The title read *Hole Hearted*. A black-and-white image of a forlorn-looking girl adorned cover.

"Please, take care of it," Priscilla said. "There aren't many copies of this book around."

"I know. I'll take good care of it, I promise. Thanks so much!" I held the book to my chest.

"So, Alfred is your English teacher?"

"Yes."

"You're very lucky. He's a very knowledgeable man."

"He's the best teacher I've ever had."

"I hope you enjoy his book. It's certainly very interesting."

"Oh, really?"

"I won't spoil it for you. To be frank, it's been a while since I read it. I only remember parts of it."

"Well, I'm looking forward to reading it." I put the book in my bag. "Is Julian around?"

Priscilla shook her head. "He's probably on his way to his life-drawing class around now."

I couldn't help feeling a tad disappointed. I had hoped we'd meet again. "Oh. Well, please tell him I said hi."

"I will. Julian told me you might come to the exhibition?"

"Yeah. I think so."

"It's opening night this Friday. Why don't you come along? I can get your name on the guest list. There'll be drinks and nibbles. Julian and I will be there."

I didn't think I had anything on, so I agreed.

"You can bring a plus one, too."

"Okay. Maybe I'll bring my friend, Lana."

"Wonderful. Julian will be thrilled you're coming!"

He will? I wondered skeptically.

Priscilla looked so pleased, I didn't say anything.

7

For the next few days, I was deeply absorbed in *Hole Hearted*. The psychological thriller had me rapt with the strange events occurring in a small town. The first scene opened with a high school girls' rowing team out on a river in the early hours of the morning. Heavy mist swirled around them.

A girl shrieked when she saw something in the water—a lifeless body floating downstream. The girls were left traumatised. When the body was recovered, they were horrified to discover it was a girl from their school.

The book had me hooked. In every spare moment, I had my head buried in it. Before school, I was so caught up in reading it, I was almost late. The bell rang just as I ran through the school gates. Seated in form class, I finally caught my breath. Through my first two classes, I struggled to concentrate. I heaved a sigh of relief when morning interval finally arrived. I met Lana outside C block, and we walked to our lockers.

"How's the book going?" she asked.

"It's awesome. I'm nearly finished."

"That was quick."

"It's not that long. Would you like to read it? I'm pretty sure Priscilla wouldn't mind."

Lana shook her head. "Just give me a précis. I don't have much time to read these days."

"Really? That sucks."

Lana shrugged. "I'll catch up on reading during the holidays."

"If you say so." I retrieved my hefty calculus textbook from my locker and transferred it to my backpack. It started to rain, so we lingered in the corridor instead of going back outside.

"The exhibition's tomorrow," Lana reminded me. "What am I going to wear?"

"Since when do you care about clothes?" Outside of school, I didn't think I'd seen her in anything other than jeans and a faded band t-shirt.

"It'll be formal, won't it? Dresses and suits and all that shit."

I couldn't believe this had not occurred to me sooner. Of course, it would be formal. *Art gallery events are posh, aren't they?*

"Yeah, I suppose it will be." My thoughts shifted to the prospect of Julian wearing a suit. I thoroughly enjoyed the mental image.

"I don't really have anything to wear to something like that."

"You can borrow something from me. I have tons of clothes." Lana and I weren't exactly the same size, her being tall and slim, and me being petite and curvy. However, I was sure I'd have something that would fit her.

"Are you sure?"

"Yeah, why not?"

"Cool."

"Why don't you come to my house after school tomorrow? We can get ready together."

"Sounds like a plan. What time does the opening start?"

"Seven. Is that okay?"

"Yeah. Should be fine. I just have a flight booked for Saturday morning, so I don't want to be up too late."

"I don't think we'll stay too late. Where are you going?"

"Auckland. I'm going to the Medical School open day."

"Oh. That's cool." That reminded me the open day for Hill University Law was coming up as well.

"Yeah. I'm pretty excited about it. Kinda nervous too. I've never been to Auckland by myself before."

"Your parents aren't going with you?"

"Nope. They need to stay and run the business. Besides, I want to prove my independence. No one goes to these things with their parents."

Well, this is quite the revelation. "Really? My mum is super keen to go to the Law School open day with me."

"Damn. You should try to talk her out of it. It's way better to go alone."

"Hmmm… I'll try that. Thanks for the tip." I wasn't sure whether it would be enough to put Mum off, but it was something to take into consideration.

After school on Friday, Lana and I raided my wardrobe and drawers, trying to pick outfits for the night. Finding something that would work for Lana proved tougher than I imagined.

I held up a silk t-shirt dress to her.

"That's super cute, but I think it'll be too short on me." She tried it on anyway, confirming the dress rode too far up her thighs.

She had almost tried on every dress in my wardrobe. Finally, something fit. The black cotton tank dress looked cute on her.

"Success!" Lana cried. She turned in front of the mirror. "But it's a little too casual, don't ya think?"

"Hmmm…you're right. But we can always dress it up a bit. A belt, some jewellery?"

"Yeah. That'll work."

I tried on the silver-coloured wrap dress I had picked out earlier, but I wasn't sure about it.

"You *have* to wear that," Lana said. "You look amazing."

"Do you think so?" I examined myself in the floor-length mirror. "You don't think it makes me look too…*busty*?"

"Well, it shows them off, but that's a good thing. You have an amazing figure."

"I'm self-conscious. I wish I had nice, small boobs."

"Trust me, you don't."

If I didn't settle on the silver dress, I might take all night going back and forth on what to wear, so I stuck with it. I didn't accessorise too much. A fancy pair of earrings, heels and a clutch. That was it.

We had a light dinner before getting changed into our outfits. I pulled my hair back into a loose bun at the nape of my neck. Stray strands were falling out, but I thought it looked good that way. A little sexy and undone.

Lana looked so different in a dress. I hadn't seen her wear one before, except at the school ball.

My parents sat in the lounge, watching television.

"Can I have the car keys?" I asked Dad.

"Sure thing, darling. Have fun tonight." He handed them over.

"Don't be too late. I'll wait up until you get home," Mum said.

I groaned. "You don't have to do that."

Dad yawned. "Well, I, for one, will be in bed at nine thirty on the dot."

Mum glared at him but said nothing.

"Let's go," I said to Lana.

She nodded, and off we went.

We arrived at the gallery on the outskirts of town. The two-storey building overlooked a tree-lined park. People milled around outside on the footpath. A man at the door was only letting a few people in at a time. We stood around in the vague queue. I felt like we stuck out among all the arty types.

Lana and I shuffled our way up the queue as others stood around talking. We stood before a stern looking man at the door. He looked us up and down with narrowed eyes. I started to sweat, feeling like we must look so out of place.

"I'm Ivy Beckett," I said quietly.

The man scanned a list for my name. When he let us in, I exhaled with relief. Through the door, we followed the sound of chatter and ascended a staircase into the gallery. The room was small, with white walls and pictures in metal frames. I wondered where Priscilla and Julian were. A quick scan around the room didn't reveal their location.

"So, what now?" Lana asked.

"There are too many people. I can't see properly." I had to raise my voice over all the loud talking.

We stood around awkwardly for a while, then someone called out, "Ivy! Lana!" The voice was neither Priscilla nor Julian.

We turned around. To my bewilderment, it was Mr. Donaldson, a glass of champagne in his hand. He had shaved and wore a navy suit. I thought he actually cleaned up quite well.

"Mr. Donaldson," I spluttered. "What are you doing here?" Despite how much I liked him, it was still awkward to bump into teachers in public.

"I could ask the same of you. I didn't know you were connected to the art scene here in our small town?"

"Someone invited me. His art is on display tonight."

"Is that so? Who is he?"

"His name is Julian."

"So, you're acquainted with Julian Hammond? Interesting."

I wondered how he knew Julian, then it hit me. "Oh yeah, you're a friend of Priscilla, aren't you?"

"So, you know Priscilla as well? You're full of surprises. And you, Lana?"

"I'm just tagging along with Ivy. I don't know anyone here," Lana explained.

"Well, I wish you both an enjoyable evening. Young Julian is a talented artist. You're sure to enjoy his work."

I nodded. "I'm curious to see what his art is like. He must be good."

"He is indeed. His display is over there by those sculptures. Go take a look."

"Thanks."

"You're welcome." He bowed curtly and disappeared back into the crowd.

Lana and I headed towards Julian's pictures. We couldn't get to the front, but I had a decent view over the shoulder of the woman in front of me.

I counted seven of his pictures all together. The beautiful portraits were rendered in a classical style. Two were nude ladies, and one was a nude male. The rest were all of the same young woman, clothed and in various poses. In the first, she sat at a piano—the one at Opulence, I realised. In the others, she sat outside a café, laid on a couch, and walked with an umbrella.

The longer I stared at the pictures, the more the familiarity of the girl sunk in. "I know her..."

"She does look familiar," Lana said. "I can't work out where I know her from."

"You know her too?"

Lana nodded.

We stood there, taking in the beauty of Julian's work.

"These are amazing," Lana mused.

"They are, aren't they?" I sighed. He was so talented. My writing was nothing compared to his art.

A laugh interrupted our quiet observation.

"This is so weird."

We turned around. The girl from Julian's drawings approached us. Charlotte, the girl I had seen at the second-hand bookstore. She was dressed in a dark green dress, and her reddish hair was tied up in a topknot.

"Pictures of me in a gallery. He's lucky I let him submit these."

"Charlotte Preston?" Lana ventured.

The girl nodded but seemed to struggle to recall Lana.

"We took piano lessons with Susanne Brady."

Charlotte smiled. "That's right. That was a few years ago. I'm sorry, but I don't remember your name."

"Lana."

"And you?" Charlotte eyed me up and down. "I saw you talking to Julian at the bookstore."

"Yes, that was me. I'm Ivy."

"How do you know Julian?"

"I don't, really. Just know him from Priscilla's shop." I was dying to know what Charlotte's relationship with Julian was, but I was scared to know the answer. My inner turmoil made me miss the opportunity to ask.

"Where are Julian and Priscilla, anyway?" Lana asked. "I still haven't met them."

"They're around. Priscilla is over there talking to Woody Anderson, Julian's art teacher."

She pointed to where I saw a glimpse of Priscilla's long black hair and a scruffy yet handsome man.

"And Julian, he's been cornered by Gilly Black, Priscilla's friend and a big admirer of his. It'll probably be some time before he's able to get away. I wonder if I should go rescue him? Nah. I'll let him suffer for a bit longer. I'm going to get another drink. Do either of you want anything?"

"Do they have anything non-alcoholic? I'm driving," I explained.

"I'm sure they have lemonade."

"That'll be fine."

"And you?" Charlotte asked Lana.

"I'll have whatever you're having."

"One lemonade and one mojito coming up."

While Charlotte went to get the drinks, Lana and I continued to look at Julian's pictures. The crowd had thinned now, and we could get a better view.

A small white plaque next to one of the pictures gave a short bio.

Julian Claude Francis Hammond, 20

Julian is an up-and-coming artist with immense talent. He graduated from Kent College, the top pupil in his year. Since then, he has been under Woody Anderson's tutelage while preparing for an apprenticeship with master draughtsman Alberto Barsetti. In Barsetti's atelier in Florence, Italy, Julian will further his draughtsmanship, as well as learn about traditional printing techniques such as engraving and etching.

My jaw dropped. "He's…so accomplished. I can't believe it."

"Alberto Barsetti? I don't know who that is, but he sounds important," Lana said.

"So, he's going to Florence? I wonder when that will be?"

Charlotte came back with the drinks.

"Thanks," I said. I felt guilty for my original judgement of Charlotte. She was actually very nice.

Priscilla made her way towards us in a cloud of heavy perfume. She looked stunning, dressed in a kimono style dress, with her hair flowing down to her waist and her lips painted dark red.

"Good evening ladies. So glad you made it. What do you think of Julian's work?"

"These are really impressive," I said.

"I'm glad you think so," Priscilla turned to Lana. "I don't believe we've met."

"Nice to meet you," Lana said. She went to shake Priscilla's hand but was greeted with a kiss on the cheek instead.

"Charmed," Priscilla said.

She also gave Charlotte a small nod of acknowledgement, and Charlotte returned a wry smile.

"I'm glad you're here, Ivy. Julian will be glad to see you."

"Does he even know I'm here? I haven't seen him all night."

"He's been inundated by various people. This whole networking thing makes him uncomfortable."

"Oh. I see."

"You must talk with him later, though, when things have quietened down. You might not be able to get a word in at this time."

"Fair enough."

"I'm glad I got to see you again, Ivy. I wanted to tell you how talented you are."

"Talented?"

"Your writing. I read your story in Alfred's newsletter."

My face flushed.

"Are you working on anything else at the moment?"

I shook my head.

"That's a shame. You shouldn't let talent like that go to waste."

I didn't say anything, just shuffled my feet in embarrassment.

"Anyway, I'll leave you to it. Make sure you have a proper look around the gallery. There is so much great art on display. Whoever knew there were so many fantastic artists in this small town?"

I nodded.

Priscilla smiled and bid us farewell. Charlotte slipped away too. I saw her chatting and flirting with the roguish Woody Anderson. I wished I had her confidence.

"What do you know about Charlotte?" I asked Lana.

"Not that much. She went to Mansfield College. She's a few years old than us. Let's see... She was head girl, three years ago, I think."

That would make her around twenty or twenty-one. "I wonder if she's Julian's girlfriend?"

Lana shrugged. "I still haven't met the guy."

We spent a while making our way slowly around the rest of the gallery. Several paintings, photographs and sculptures were displayed. I noted which pieces were Woody's. His art was bold and abstract. Nothing like Julian's classic style.

The gallery had quietened down significantly. I couldn't see Julian anywhere. I checked the time and realised we needed to leave soon. As eager as Lana was to meet Julian, I could tell she was getting bored. I thought it better not to make her linger too much longer.

"Let's head off," I said.

"What about Julian?"

I shrugged. "He's not around. It's fine."

"It's not fine."

"It's fine. Really."

"Well, all right." She didn't put up much of a fight. "I just need to use the bathroom, and then we can go."

I nodded. Lana disappeared down the corridor. Across the room, a floor-length curtain fluttered in the breeze, revealing a glimpse of the outdoors beyond it.

It must lead to a balcony.

I decided to slip out for a minute to get some fresh air.

There, on the balcony, was Julian, dressed in a grey suit with a navy tie. He held a glass of red wine and stared out over the park. He looked solemn, like he wanted to be left alone.

"Oh, I'm sorry," I squeaked and turned to leave. A hand came down on my shoulder, stopping me.

"It's okay." His voice was soft and deep.

My knees weakened.

"I just wanted a moment alone, but it's okay if it's you."

"Oh?"

"As long as you don't interrogate me."

"What do you mean?"

"I get asked the same questions, over and over, about my art and future plans. It gets pretty tiring."

"Well, I promise I won't do that. I just came outside to get some fresh air." I crossed the balcony and looked out over the edge. It was a calm, cool night. The moonlight gave the town park a beautiful glow. I took slow, deep breaths of the brisk night air.

After a moment of silence, Julian spoke. "Thanks for coming out tonight. I wasn't sure if you'd make it."

"Well, I'm here. I like your work. You're a really good artist."

"Thanks," he said, avoiding eye contact.

My phone buzzed in my pocket. I pulled it out to see a message from Lana. *Where are you?*

"Sorry, I need to go. My friend's waiting for me."

Julian nodded. "Actually, I'd better get back in there too, before people assume I've abandoned the place."

I pulled back the curtain and returned to the gallery. Julian followed me. Lana sat on a couch. She stood up when I approached her with Julian still at my side.

"Julian, this is my friend Lana. Lana, Julian."

"Hey," Lana said, her eyes searching him. She seemed pleased by what she saw.

"Nice to meet you, Lana."

"We loved seeing your art. Your drawings are so good."

"Thank you."

"Is Charlotte Preston your muse?"

Julian seemed taken aback. "You know Charlotte?"

"Yes. Not well, but I was kinda surprised to see her in your drawings."

"Muse might be too strong a word. It can be pretty tough to find willing models outside my drawing class. Thankfully, Charlotte volunteered."

I tried not to let my relief show.

"Actually, with Charlotte going back to uni in a few days, I'm going to be model-less. I have a portfolio due soon, so it's not great timing. I don't know what I'm gonna do."

"That sucks," I said. "I hope you manage to find someone."

Lana looked thoughtful. "What about Ivy?"

"What?" I spluttered.

Outside of Julian's view, Lana gave me a gentle nudge. "I'm too busy myself, but Ivy has time, and she'd be a great model."

"I don't know about that…"

Julian looked me up and down, assessing me. "I think you'd be perfect."

"See, Julian thinks so too. So, why not?"

Every cell in my body wanted to shout, "no way," but this was my chance to spend more time with Julian. Could I try not to screw it up? I just had one concern.

"This would all be fully clothed, right?"

"Yes," Julian said, his face reddening. "I only draw nude models in my drawing class."

It took another moment of consideration, but then I agreed. "Well, all right, then. If you need me."

"Are you sure?" Julian asked with caution.

I nodded.

"Thanks, Ivy. I already have your number. I'll be in touch."

Oh, my God. What had I just signed up for?

"Right, well, we'd better get going," I said, half choking.

"Bye, Julian," Lana said with a smile. "Nice to meet you."

"Have a good night." Julian looked at me. "Bye, Ivy."

"Bye," I croaked. My face grew red, so I tugged Lana out the door with me.

As soon as we were out of earshot, Lana blurted, "He's gorgeous. Even I think so." She was almost as giddy as I was.

"Why did you volunteer me to be his model?"

"What? It's the perfect opportunity for the two of you to get closer. You'll thank me later."

I sighed. "I hope you're right." It was too late to back out now.

8

I woke to my phone buzzing and groaned. *Who in their right mind would text me at this hour?* I blindly outstretched my arm and felt for the phone on my bedside table. Once it was safely within my grasp, I pulled it towards me, and through bleary eyes, I read the message.

Thanks for coming out last night. J.

My heart did a somersault in my chest. Suddenly, I was wide awake. Checking the time, I realised it wasn't so early after all. It was already after ten. I staggered out of bed, and after a quick shower, I went to make breakfast.

"Good afternoon," Mum said upon my entrance. "How kind of you to grace us with your presence."

"Good morning to you too," I bit back.

"Morning, honey," Dad said from out on the patio. "How was the exhibition?"

"It was fantastic. I never realised there was such an art scene here." I went to the kitchen and popped two slices of bread in the toaster. "Cup of tea?" I asked Mum as I filled the kettle.

"Oh, yes please," she replied.

When the toast was done and the tea had brewed, I brought a tray over to the table. I placed a cup of tea on a coaster next to Mum, who sat with her laptop in front of her.

"Look at this!" Mum said.

"What is it?" I took a bite of the Nutella-smothered toast.

"There's a sale on flights to Wellington for the days the Law School open day is on."

"Oh?"

"Shall I go ahead and book tickets for us? These deals sell out fast."

"That might be a good idea, Ivy," Dad said, coming over to have a look for himself. He squinted at the laptop screen. "I've never seen fares cheaper than this."

I thought about what Lana had said about going by herself. With a small breath, I uttered, "Are you coming too?"

Mum looked confused. "Why wouldn't I?"

"I heard most students go by themselves."

"Really? But, surely, most parents are interested in going too?"

"It's just that it looks better to go on your own. It shows you're independent."

"Ivy has a point," Dad chimed in. "I suppose it's sort of like turning up to apply for a job and having your mother in tow."

Mum was rendered speechless. After a while, she gathered her words. "Well, I never thought of it that way."

"You're all grown up now, Ivy. I think it would be good for you to go on your own. You don't need your mother holding your hand."

"I'll be fine," I assured Mum.

She crossed her arms. I could tell she was still working it out in her head. "Hmmm. Okay, then," she finally said. "I could still go with you and just stay behind while you're at the open day."

"I don't think that's really necessary."

"You're sure you'll be fine?"

I nodded. "I'll be there all on my own next year. Might as well get a taste of it now."

"All right. You can book the flight yourself, then. I'll leave it all to you."

She was in a huff now, but it was well worth it.

"I can book it. I'll need money, though."

Dad pulled out his wallet and took out a credit card. "Here," he said, handing it over. "Go crazy."

"Thanks."

"You might as well book accommodation while you're at it."

"Don't spend too much," Mum warned. "You're just there for one night."

"I won't!"

In my room, I booted up the computer and promptly booked the discounted plane tickets. Only then did it sink in that I'd be going by myself. Complete freedom for a weekend. I did a little research on decent budget hotels before booking a single room at the Travelodge. I also booked airport transfers for convenience's sake. With each booking confirmation, I grew more excited. It would be the first time I'd ever gone out of town by myself.

In the thrill of it all, I forgot about Julian's text message. I didn't remember to reply until later on in the day. Reading over his message once again, I typed my reply and hit send.

No problem. I had a good time.

A few seconds later, his reply came. *Still keen to do some modelling? Let me know if you have changed your mind.*

I was tempted to say I was having second thoughts. Just picturing myself as a model made me cringe with embarrassment. But I thought about what Lana told me. It's a good opportunity to get closer to him. I took a deep breath and replied.

I haven't changed my mind. Let me know when you want me.

Julian answered, and we worked out a time. On Thursday afternoon, he would draw me. The gravity of the situation was not lost on me.

I set out to Opulence on Thursday. When I arrived, a sign on the door read, *Back soon*. I peered through the window. The shop was empty, but I knocked anyway. I had arrived a little early, so it was understandable if Julian hadn't expected me yet. Standing there, waiting with my arms folded, I grew increasingly anxious. Eventually, footsteps approached and the door opened.

"Hi," Julian said, seeming a little flustered. He wore a white apron covered in smudges of charcoal and graphite. His shirt sleeves were rolled up, revealing subtly muscular arms, and a pencil was tucked behind his ear.

"Sorry. Didn't realise Priscilla left. I thought the shop was open."

"That's okay. I wasn't waiting long."

"Good." He stood aside. "Come on in."

I followed him across the shop floor, behind the beaded curtain, around the corner and to the narrow, impossibly steep staircase. Memories of the fateful afternoon I'd ended up here during the storm flooded back. I had been so curious to get a better look inside the studio.

Now, here I was. The large, airy room stood before me. The main feature was the large, sloping drawing desk in front of the window. Then there were bookshelves containing volume upon volume of reference books. Small tables and stools were scattered around, splattered in paint and ink. Stacks of paper and jars full of paintbrushes sat atop shelves and tabletops. The room pulsed with creative energy.

"I can't believe you've got your own space like this," I said. "It would be my dream to have a room like this to work on my own. Complete privacy. Peace and quiet. My mum doesn't even like me closing the door to my room. She thinks it's rude."

Julian chuckled. "I'm very lucky. Priscilla lets me use this room for free. Otherwise, I'd never be able to afford a studio space like this."

"Has she always let you use it?"

He shook his head. "Only after I finished school. That was when I decided to start taking my art more seriously."

"Makes sense. Did you always know you wanted to be an artist?"

"Not really. Art was just a hobby for me, but one day, I realised it could be my career, and I went with it."

I wandered around the room, taking it all in while Julian set up an easel and a stool. He sharpened a selection of pencils with a rotary sharpener and put a fresh canvas on the easel. After that, he positioned a small, wooden chair a short distance from the easel. I assumed that's where I'd be sitting.

"I'm going to put some music on. Hope you don't mind," Julian said.

"Not at all." In fact, it relieved me to no end that we wouldn't have to sit in silence.

"It helps get me in the zone. Maybe it will help you relax too."

Is my nervousness that obvious?

Julian took a CD from a stack on the floor and put it in the stereo. He pushed play and Mozart filled the room.

"I can't concentrate if the music has lyrics," he explained, moving back towards the easel. "Shall we begin?"

I nodded.

He gestured towards the chair. "Take a seat. Let's start off simple. Just sit normally. No pose required."

"Right."

"Make sure you're comfortable. You'll be sitting there for a while."

I relaxed, giving in to my natural slouch.

"Great."

He sat at the easel. For what seemed like an eternity, he stared at me. His gaze was so intense. I prayed he didn't notice me shake with nervousness. Sweat gathered at my hairline. Finally, he took a pencil in his hand and began to draw.

It surprised me how little he looked at the canvas. For the majority of the time, his eyes were fixated on me. Scanning my minutiae. I felt uncomfortable at first, but eventually, I tuned out. The classical music helped a lot.

The afternoon light was fading when Julian got up and turned on the light. "Let's take a break."

I stood up and stretched. My back clicked.

"Are you okay?"

"Fine. Thank you. Just a bit stiff."

"Would you like a glass of water?"

"Yes, please."

Julian went downstairs. While he was gone, I cautiously

stole a glance at his drawing. It was still mostly a basic outline, with only a few portions shaded in. Julian came back shortly with two glasses of water. When we had refreshed ourselves, I sat back down, and he returned to work. I felt much more at ease.

Darkness had set in by the time Julian announced we could call it a day. He eyed the canvas in front of him but didn't look too enthused about his work.

"Can I have a look?" I asked.

Julian didn't answer straight away. I wondered if he were embarrassed. What right did he have to be embarrassed, anyway? I was the embarrassed one about this whole ordeal. Although, I had to admit it had been significantly less mortifying than I'd thought it would be.

"I don't normally like showing people works in progress. I'm kind of anal about things like that. But since you did me this huge favour, I kind of owe it to you, don't I?"

I sighed. "You don't have to show me if you don't want to." Truthfully, I was desperate to see. I couldn't tell anything from the bare outline I'd glimpsed earlier.

"It's fine." He gestured for me to come to his side.

I looked at the picture. My face had been rendered in meticulous detail. I looked much prettier than I expected I would. Perhaps that's why Julian seemed unsatisfied—it wasn't realistic enough. Nevertheless, it was the start of a beautiful portrait. The neck and the shoulders were drawn in detail, but going down from there, the rest of my body was a faint sketch. A tangle of lines with no proper shading.

"See what I mean?" Julian said. "It doesn't look all that great."

"Are you kidding? It's wonderful."

"It still needs a lot of work."

"Yeah, but it already looks so good."

"You think so?"

"Absolutely."

"I might need you to come in again, just so I can finish off a few details."

"That's fine. Same time next week?"

"That would work. Thanks so much for your help today."

"No problem at all."

Julian walked me down the stairs and back into the shop.

Priscilla was there, tidying and organising the shelves. "How did you two get on?" she asked.

"It went well," Julian replied.

"That's good. Ivy, do you have any plans for this evening? I thought we could all get something to eat."

My stomach rumbled at the very mention of food. My parents probably expected me home for dinner, but I couldn't resist taking Priscilla up on her offer. "Sure. Sounds good."

"Wonderful." Priscilla smiled. "There's a great little Thai place down the road that does takeaways. I'll phone in now and place an order."

After Priscilla ordered our meal, Julian left to pick it up. Priscilla and I sat down in the kitchen.

"Did you finish reading the book I lent you?" Priscilla asked.

"Oh! I almost forgot." I rummaged through my backpack and produced the copy of *Hole Hearted*. "I finished it last weekend."

"What did you think about it?"

"It was strange. Moody, atmospheric. I liked it a lot."

"Alfred sure has a brilliant imagination."

"I'd like to read more of his work."

"This is his only book, I'm afraid."

"I wonder why he didn't write any more books?"

"I don't know," Priscilla said ruefully. "He is a man of great talent. I'm sure he has many more stories to tell."

"Maybe he's just writing in secret."

"Great art deserves to be shared."

"I suppose so." I sighed. "Anyway, thanks for letting me borrow the book. I know how precious it is."

"You're welcome, my dear."

I was about to hand it over when I remembered someone else wished to read it. "Priscilla, would it be okay if I lent it to my friend Anna? She's the school librarian and has always wanted to read it."

"Yes. I suppose that would be okay as long as you trust she'll take good care of it."

"I don't know anyone who cares more for books than Anna."

Priscilla smiled. "Very well, then. Return it to me when she's done."

"I will. Thank you." I tucked the book away again.

Julian came back momentarily, carrying two plastic bags stacked with takeaway cartons.

"Let's eat," Priscilla said.

We huddled around the kitchen table and dug in. I was ravenous.

"So, Ivy, how was your first time as an artist's model?" Priscilla asked between mouthfuls.

"It wasn't as awful as I thought it would be."

Julian grinned. "Come on, it wasn't awful at all."

"I was so anxious. Could you tell?"

"Don't worry. I was anxious too."

"You were?"

Julian nodded.

"He's a perfectionist. He worries far too much about his work," Priscilla explained.

Julian shot her a glare. "I just like to do the best I can."

I sighed deeply. Julian was so committed to his art. I wondered what it felt like to be so passionate about something.

"You look wistful. What's on your mind?" Priscilla asked.

"I was just thinking about how wonderful it must be to be an artist."

"It's hard work, just like anything else," Julian said.

"But you're doing what you want to do."

Julian nodded. "I can't imagine doing anything else."

"It must be nice..."

"Growing up, I was always taught you can do anything you want to as long as you set your mind to it."

Priscilla nodded. "I think that's true as well. Too bad I didn't know that when I was your age. I made so many terrible choices. Luckily, I pulled through in the end." She turned to me. "Ivy, what do you want to do?"

I blushed, suddenly embarrassed. *Lawyer*, I thought, but it felt like such a lie. "I don't know," I confessed.

Priscilla smiled kindly. "There's still plenty of time to figure it out."

I nodded. "I'm sure I'll work it out."

When we had finished eating, I helped Priscilla clear up. "Thanks so much for dinner."

"You're welcome," Priscilla said.

"Do you need a ride home?" Julian asked.

I checked my watch. "I can wait for the bus."

"Let me give you a ride. It's late."

"Well, okay, then. Thank you."

After saying goodbye to Priscilla, I followed Julian outside. He unlocked a gate at the side of the building. A motorcycle was parked at the back. He passed me a helmet.

"A motorcycle?" I asked, stunned.

"Are you okay with that?"

"My parents would definitely disapprove of this."

"So, it's a no?"

I shook my head. "It's a yes."

"You're a rebel." Julian chuckled.

No, not at all. But, tonight, all my cares were out the window.

"What's your address?"

"27 Dalton Place."

Julian got on the motorcycle, and I clambered on behind him.

"Is this your first time on a motorcycle?" he asked.

"Yes."

"Put your arms around my waist."

"Like this?"

"Yes. Don't be afraid to hold on tight." He started the motor. "Here we go."

Before I could change my mind, we were off.

As we zoomed down the street, the air rushing past us, I felt like we were flying. I had never felt so free before. It was exhilarating.

When Julian stopped at the bottom of my driveway, I was disappointed it was over so soon. I let go of his waist and got down.

"Thanks for the lift."

"That's all right."

"Goodnight."

"Night. See you next week."

I walked up the driveway. When I arrived on the doorstep, I looked over my shoulder. Julian was still there, waiting for me to go inside. I gave him a wave before I opened the door. When I entered, I was faced by my glaring parents.

"Ivy, I want a word with you," Dad said.

9

"What is it?" I asked with a sigh of aggravation.

"You know the rules, Ivy. If you're not going to be home for dinner, you need to let us know."

"I told you I didn't know what time I would get back."

"That's not the point."

"But, more importantly," Mum chimed in, "what were you doing on a motorbike?"

"I was offered a lift home. The next bus wasn't going to be for another forty minutes—"

"You know my thoughts on motorbikes. They're dangerous."

"The roads were quiet. It was completely fine."

"We decide what's fine and what isn't."

"Whatever," I grumbled and started towards my room.

"Don't speak to me in that tone, young lady."

I took a deep breath in the safety of my room. *They'll get over it.*

~

I kept my head down over the next few days. If I put a foot wrong, my parents could ban me from seeing Julian and Priscilla again. I wouldn't put it past them.

Like a good girl, I dedicated my attention to the pile of accumulating assignments taking over my desk. Next up, economics.

When the OCR is decreased, what is the effect on inflation?

I knew we had gone over this several times in class, but the answer didn't surface. I thought harder. Nothing. I was feeling lazy, so I turned to Google. A few results popped up. I clicked on the first one and began to read. The dense and technical wall of text made my mind drift. I didn't care about any of this.

Why am I even taking economics in the first place? I hate it. It's boring. Oh, that's right. My parents made me take it. It's practical, they said. It's a useful subject to know. I groaned. Why couldn't I do what I wanted to do for once, completely disregarding practicality?

I thought of Julian in his studio, creating works of art. How wonderful it must be to pursue a dream like that.

I put aside my economics assignment. It had been such a long time since I wrote anything for pleasure. I should have been dutifully working on my assignments, but the urge to write took over. I decided I might as well embrace it.

I dug around in my desk drawer and found an old notebook. In it, were several old story ideas and partly written pieces. I read through the first page and then the next. Before I knew it, I had read the whole notebook. Some of it was actually pretty good. I even laughed to myself from time to time.

I turned to the next fresh page and jotted down the first few ideas that came to my head. Feeling inspired, I let myself write freely. Utter drivel, but it felt good to put something down on paper.

Despite getting hardly any work done on my assignments, I went to bed feeling fulfilled and with a new sense of resolve.

In my free period the next day, I decided to drop in and see Mr. Donaldson in his office. Perhaps he could give me some advice. Down the back corridor in A Block, there was a door with a small metal plaque attached which read *English Department*. I went inside and found Mr. Donaldson's room easily enough. He was the Head of Department, so his room was the largest. I peeked my head around the door. He was sitting at his desk, his glasses on, a stack of papers in front of him and a red pen in his hand.

"Mr. Donaldson?" I asked, drawing his attention.

"Ivy."

He looked a little shocked to see me. Maybe he wasn't used to students coming to see him in his office.

"Do come in."

I sat down in the chair opposite his desk.

Mr. Donaldson put his pen down and his papers aside, giving me his full attention. "What can I do for you?"

"I wanted to ask you a few things if you don't mind."

"Certainly. Go on."

"Well…" I fidgeted nervously. "I wondered if you had any feedback about my story in your newsletter."

Mr. Donaldson smiled. "You're very brave."

I blushed.

"There hasn't been much feedback, but from what I've heard, the reaction to your story was quite positive."

"Really?" I exhaled in relief. "That's good."

"I wish I could tell you more. The newsletter isn't exactly a platform for critique."

"That's okay. I was just curious. That's all."

"Anything else?"

I nodded. "I wanted to ask your advice about getting better at writing."

Mr. Donaldson's blue eyes lit up. "I must say, I'm very glad to hear this. So, you've decided to take your writing more seriously?"

I shrugged. "I want to give it a shot."

"First and foremost, I would urge you to write every day."

"Every day?"

Mr. Donaldson nodded. "You need not produce a masterpiece. Just something. Even if it's terrible. It all helps in the end."

"Okay. So, I need to write every day."

"I could also recommend some excellent reference books."

"That would be helpful."

He bent down and opened a desk drawer. He retrieved a notepad and scribbled down a list of titles. "Start with these. You should be able to get them from the library." He tore off the sheet and handed it to me.

"Thanks."

"Oh, and if you ever want a critique of a piece, I would be happy to provide my expertise."

"Thanks. I'm sure I'll take you up on that."

"Please do. I'm just delighted you're doing this, Ivy. I meant what I said before. You're a very talented writer. Ever since your first year in my class, I've enjoyed your work."

"Thank you."

"Oh, and one more thing. Have you considered taking a creative writing course next year?"

"No. Not really."

"There's no shortage of great programmes. If you're truly serious about writing, perhaps you should look into it."

"Thanks. I will," I lied. It would be completely out of the question. Nevertheless, I was pleased with Mr. Donaldson's encouragement and enthusiasm.

I headed straight to the library to see if they had any of the books he'd recommended.

When I arrived, Anna welcomed me. "Hey, Ivy. How's it going?"

"I'm good, thanks. And you? You must be close to your due date now?"

Anna nodded. "Sure am. Only three weeks to go. I'm going on leave next week."

"That's good. Must be getting pretty uncomfortable for you."

"It's all right, but I'll be able to relax much more at home."

"How long are you off for?"

"Six months, at least."

"I'm going to miss you."

Anna laughed. "You'll be fine. Besides, you can come visit me whenever you want."

"Really? I'd like that."

"And Ms. Tate will be taking over the library while I'm gone. She was the librarian here before I started."

I sighed. "It won't be the same without you."

"Don't be so dramatic."

"Remember the first time we met?"

Anna nodded. "How could I forget? It was your first day of

high school and my first day at a proper job. We were so nervous."

When I first started at Bridgeway High, Lana went to another school at the time. I didn't have any friends, so I often hid out at the library. That's how I became so close with Anna.

"Anyway, what brings you here today? Looking for anything in particular?" Anna asked.

"Yes, actually." I produced the list of books Mr. Donaldson gave me.

Anna took the piece of paper and ran her eyes over it. "Writing books? How interesting."

"I would like to try taking it more seriously. Mr. Donaldson recommended these books."

"So, you want to be a writer?"

I shrugged. "I don't know. I just want to have a go at it."

"Well, I hope it goes well. Please let me read some of your work."

"Only if I manage to write something half-decent."

"Of course, you will. Now, let's see. I think we have most of these…" Anna looked the books up on the computer. "You're in luck. We have all of them but one, and they're all available."

"Really? Great!"

Anna directed me to the appropriate section of the library. "If there's anything you can't find, let me know."

"Thanks, Anna."

I spent several minutes methodically searching the shelves and picking out the books I wanted. With my arms full, I returned to the issues desk.

"Are you sure you can carry all these?" Anna asked when I plonked them down on the desk.

"It's fine. I can keep some in my locker."

As Anna scanned the books through, it occurred to me I

hadn't given her *Hole Hearted* yet. I retrieved the copy from my bag. "I forgot to lend you this."

"Oh? What is it?" Anna asked, taking a closer look.

"It's Mr. Donaldson's book."

Anna gasped. "How on earth did you manage to get this?" She took the book in her hands and examined it, turning it over and over.

"Through a friend of Mr. Donaldson."

"Can I really borrow this?"

"Yes, but take care of it."

"I promise to keep it in good condition. Thanks, Ivy. I'll let you know when I'm done with it."

I headed to Opulence on Thursday for my next modelling session. The stairs creaked as I ascended to Julian's studio. Now that I knew what to expect, I was much less nervous about modelling. Julian sat at his desk, sharpening all his pencils. The last of the afternoon light filtered in through the window, bathing him in a golden glow. He looked almost angelic.

"Hi, Ivy. How's it going?" He turned to face me.

"It's been an interesting week."

"What happened?"

"Seeing you work on your art, it inspired me."

A smile played on Julian's lips. "Really? What are you working on?"

I blushed, suddenly embarrassed. "I want to become a better writer."

"Oh, yeah. Priscilla told me you're a writer. I'd like to read your work."

"It's not that great."

"Priscilla said you were good."

"Really?"

Julian nodded.

"I feel like I need to improve."

"There's always room for improvement. Nobody's perfect."

"Yeah. I suppose you're right."

Julian got to his feet. "Shall we get started?"

I nodded and positioned myself the same as last time. I had even remembered to wear the same clothes. Julian sat behind the easel, and I tried to remain calm under the intensity of his green-eyed gaze. Heat rose to my cheeks and my vision swirled. Eventually, the classical music in the background relaxed me, and I was away in my thoughts.

This session went much faster than the last. Before I knew it, Julian was telling me to get up.

"That's all I need. I can do the rest without a model."

"Oh." I was surprisingly disappointed. "Will you need me again at all?"

"I think so. My final portfolio isn't quite ready. I still need more practice."

"Well, just text me whenever you need someone."

Julian nodded.

I grabbed my bag, readying myself to leave.

"Ivy," Julian began.

"Yes?"

"You've been a lot of help. I want… I want to pay you back somehow."

"Oh. It's okay. I don't want anything in return."

Julian hesitated. "How about I take you out for lunch one day? My treat."

Caught off-guard, I struggled to formulate a reply.

Julian continued. "There's this new café on Bryant Place. I've been meaning to go there for ages. I'd love to take you."

Did my ears deceive me? He had even used the word *love*. "That sounds nice," I said, trying to sound as nonchalant as possible.

"So, you'll come? Is Saturday okay?"

"Yeah, suits me."

"Okay. See you Saturday."

I tried to stay calm, but on the inside, I was dancing with joy.

10

I approached Bryant Place, my stomach churning with nerves. My sense of joy at having lunch with Julian had turned into trepidation. This was my chance to try to make a good impression. I begged myself to try not to stuff it up.

The sun shone in the clear sky. I wore a sweater and a denim skirt with tights and boots. It had taken me ages to settle on this outfit. Cute but not dressed up. I dawdled along, still several minutes early. The café came into view.

You can do this, Ivy. With a gulp of air, I entered.

The café was a long and narrow room, windowless except at the entrance, giving the place a cave-like feel. The walls were exposed brick, and there were indoor plants all around—hanging from the ceiling and crawling over the walls. Saxophone music played. My eyes scanned the room, but I didn't see Julian. I grabbed a magazine from the rack and took a seat. I flipped through it mindlessly, keeping one eye on the café entrance.

Julian arrived a couple minutes late, wearing jeans and a

button-down shirt with the sleeves rolled up. He didn't appear flustered at all, unlike me. Our eyes met, and he walked over.

"Hey. Hope you weren't waiting too long."

"No. For some reason, I have a habit of arriving early. It's no problem."

I put the magazine away while Julian settled in his seat.

"This is a cute place."

"Yeah." Julian looked around the room. "It's even nicer than I thought it would be."

"Thanks for taking me."

"That's okay."

"How did you find out about this café?"

"I walk past it all the time."

"But you never went in?"

"Yeah. I don't know why. My parents were really into dining and used to take me out all the time. I don't really eat out much anymore since they left."

"Oh, really? Where did your parents go?"

"They're in France."

"What are they doing there? Are they on holiday?"

"They live there now. They're restoring an old chateau in Bordeaux."

I couldn't help but sigh. It sounded so romantic. "That's really cool. I mean, it sucks they left you. You didn't want to go with them?"

"I could have if I wanted to, but I knew I'd get more work done if I just stayed here. I'm still living in their house. They'll sell it once I've moved to Florence."

"When's the big move?" I asked, a little tentatively.

"Nothing's been confirmed yet, but most likely November. I'm going to spend Christmas in France with my parents first and then head to Italy in January."

"November? That's so soon."

"I know. Anyway, have you decided what you're going to have?"

"I haven't even looked at the menu yet." I picked up a menu from the table and read through the options, my mouth watering. "Everything looks amazing. What are you going to have?"

"The Italian bowl with chicken."

"That looks good. I might get the Spanish bowl with lamb."

"Do you want a drink?"

"An orange juice, thanks."

Julian went to the counter to order.

In his absence, I allowed myself to relax. So far, things were going pretty well. I was glad to have the opportunity to finally talk to him properly.

Julian came back to the table. "How's school going? You're in your last year, right? Must be stressful."

"Yeah. It can be. Sometimes, I feel like I'm drowning in assignments. Mock exams are just around the corner, too."

"Are you going to university next year?"

"Yeah. That's the plan. I'm going to study law at Hill University."

"Law?" Julian raised an eyebrow.

"Yeah. What's wrong with that?"

"Nothing. It's just that you never struck me as a lawyer type."

"Oh? Why not?"

Julian shrugged. "It was just a feeling."

"It's funny. Priscilla said something similar to me on the day we met."

"What did she say?"

"That she felt I had an artistic spirit."

Julian laughed. "Well, isn't she right? You're a writer, after all."

"Well, not a writer, per se."

"But you do write, don't you?"

"Yes."

"Then you're a writer."

"In a sense."

"It took me a while to call myself an artist, too."

"It's not the same. Art is, like, your career."

Julian laughed, shaking his head. "I wish it was. Actually, I have never even sold a drawing. That's why I work at Lucky Books for minimum wage and Aunty Priscilla lets me use the studio for free."

"But still—"

"You enjoy writing, don't you?"

"Yes. I love it."

"You should do what you love."

"Perhaps you're right." I sighed. "Mr. Donaldson wants me to apply to a creative writing course next year."

"That could be a good idea. Why not?"

"For a start, my parents would never let me."

"Do you really need their approval?"

"I don't think I'll be able to afford university without their help."

"You can always get a part-time job."

"Yeah, I guess." I contemplated his suggestion. I loved writing, but I always thought I shouldn't waste my time on it. It wouldn't ever lead to anything. But here was Julian, an artist with a studio and his work in galleries. He was living the kind of life I would never have dreamed possible. If he could be an artist, why couldn't I be a writer?

"If you don't mind me asking, why aren't you at university?"

"It's a long story."

"It's okay. Tell me."

"Well, all right, then."

I leaned in to listen closely.

"My original plan was to study a degree in fine arts after I finished school."

"So, what happened?"

"I visited the National Art Gallery on a school trip. That's when I discovered the work of Alberto Barsetti. I loved his art so much that I became obsessed. When I found out he was accepting students, I instantly knew that's what I wanted to do."

"So, you applied?"

Julian shook his head. "I couldn't. Each intake is five years apart."

"So, that's why you're still here…?"

"Yeah. I had to wait. But it's given me the opportunity to save up and work on my craft, and this year, I was finally able to start my application. I've already made it through the first two rounds."

"Wow, he must like your work."

Julian nodded. "Basically, I've already been accepted. As long as I get my final portfolio in on time, I should get in."

How impressive. I sighed. "I haven't even thought about studying abroad. Actually, I've never even been overseas before. Is that bad?"

"I don't think so. I'm sure that's common."

"What about you? Have you travelled?"

Julian nodded. "Extensively. My parents took my brothers and I around the world when we were kids."

"Wow…that's so cool. Must have been a wonderful childhood."

"Not really. I didn't appreciate it at all. I just wanted to be like a regular kid. Go to school and have friends."

"Ah. That would have been tough."

"Yeah, but looking back now, I realise how lucky I was. My brothers and I learnt so much more from travelling than from school."

"How old are your brothers?"

"Twenty-two and twenty-five. I don't see them much. They live overseas. Do you have any siblings?"

"No. I'm an only child."

Our lunch arrived. I took a fork and began. "When did you become interested in art?" I asked when I had finished my mouthful.

Julian shrugged. "I've always liked to draw. My parents were really encouraging too. What about you? Have you always been a writer?"

"Yes, I think so. My parents don't support it, though. It's funny because my dad actually used to be a journalist."

"Really?"

"Yeah. He still works for the newspaper, but he's in advertising sales now."

"Why did he switch to sales?"

"I don't know. The money, I suppose. I've tried to ask him about it before, but he doesn't like to talk about it. Part of me wonders if my mum had something to do with it. Maybe she pressured him into a higher paying job?"

"I'm sure there must be some other explanation."

"You don't know my mum."

"I guess not. But still…" Julian sighed.

That broke the conversation for a while. Instead, we ate,

enjoying our meals.

"I hate to have to ask, but when do you think you'll be available for another modelling session?" Julian asked when he had finished eating.

"I have a couple of assignments due next week, so I probably won't have any time. Then I'm out of town next weekend."

"Where are you going?"

"The Law School open day at Hill University."

"You might find out whether a law degree is really for you."

"Yeah. I suppose I will."

"Let me know how it goes."

"Sure."

We lingered for a while, letting our food go down. Julian checked his watch. "I should probably get going. Priscilla will be expecting me at the shop."

I swallowed my disappointment and put on a smile. "Thanks for lunch."

Julian returned the smile. "We should do it again sometime."

"Really? Sure, I'd like that," I blurted.

He opened the door for me. "I'll text you."

Later that day, I was sitting in my room and slowly working through the latest tedious assignment when my phone rang. I rushed to answer it, all too glad for the disruption.

"Hello?"

"Hi, Ivy. It's me, Anna."

I was surprised to hear her voice. She sounded cheerful. I

wondered what she could be calling about.

"Hey. How's it going?"

"Just biding my time until the baby comes. I'm practically ready to burst." She chuckled.

"How are you holding up?"

"I'm mostly confined to the couch these days. I can barely move. My husband has been waiting on me hand and foot."

"That's nice. Is he off work too?"

"No. He works from home, but I'm keeping his hands full for now. It will be even worse when the baby arrives."

"I hope it all works out."

"Thanks, Ivy. Anyway, I called because I finished *Hole Hearted*."

"Oh! What did you think?"

"It's a brilliant book, of course, but I had the strangest feeling. I felt a major sense of déjà vu."

"Hmmm… Had you read it before without realising?"

"That's what I thought at first, but I've been keeping a detailed log of every book I've read for several years now. I definitely hadn't read it before, yet I couldn't shake this feeling."

"Huh. Weird."

"I decided to investigate. I entered some passages from it into a book database to see what would come up. You'll never guess what I discovered!"

"What?"

"A book with a different title and different author popped up. *The Drifting Girl* by Alexander Morris. It was published in the UK seven years ago."

"What does that mean?"

"My theory is that, when *Hole Hearted* went out of print, Alfred must have regained the rights which he later sold to a publisher in the UK. The book then got republished under a different title and pen name."

"Is *The Drifting Girl* still in print?"

"Yes, it is, and that's not all. We thought Alfred only published one book, but if my theory is correct, Alexander Morris and Alfred Donaldson are one and the same, and there are several more books. Alexander Morris has ten titles to his name."

"That's incredible! It must be true. I knew Mr. Donaldson wouldn't give up after one book."

"Yes, I think so too. Too bad I didn't hold on to my copy of *The Drifting Girl*. It isn't easily available here, so I've ordered a copy from overseas. Hopefully, it will arrive soon. I have a gut feeling there will be answers within."

"Let me know what you find out."

"I will. In the meantime, I'll get my husband to drop off *Hole Hearted* at your house, so you can return it."

"Thanks, Anna."

"Goodnight, Ivy."

As soon as the conversation ended, I opened Google and searched *Alexander Morris*. A few results appeared, and I opened them all on new tabs. Before long, I was down a rabbit hole, trying to dig up as much detail as I could find. All it did was lead me to a dead end. I learned a lot about his books—well-reviewed psychological thrillers, but the man himself was a complete mystery.

When I realised the time, I was shocked. Almost midnight. I was none the wiser about the identity of Alexander Morris, and I had completely forgotten to pack for my trip to Wellington. I went to bed, resolving to pack in the morning.

Although I wasn't able to gain any more insight on Alexander Morris, I felt in my heart that Anna was right.

11

"Come on, Ivy. Let's get going," Dad called from the hallway.

"Coming!" I called back. I grabbed my lightly packed duffel bag off the bed and met Dad outside by the car.

He drove me to the airport. I didn't fly often, so I was nervous just for this short domestic flight.

"Passengers may begin boarding flight 2154 to Wellington," a voice said over the speaker.

Dad squeezed my hand. "Have a great time, darling. Don't do anything I wouldn't do."

I hugged him. "See you tomorrow."

I joined the queue. When I reached the front, I presented my boarding pass. Then I was out on the tarmac and waving to Dad before boarding the little 737.

I stuffed my duffel bag into the overhead locker. After take off, I shut my eyes, lay back and listened to my iPod. Before I knew it, the plane was being prepared for landing.

A short taxi ride later, I arrived at the hotel. My room was small but modern and clean. I lay on the bed, luxuriating in the crisp white bedding. I texted Mum to say I had arrived safe and sound. After a few moments of relaxation, I decided to hit the town and orientate myself. After all, this city would be my home next year. It would be good to familiarise myself with it. I didn't have a map, so I traced my steps with care.

The city had a claustrophobic feel, with tall, tight buildings lining the hilly streets. Cafés were tucked into every corner, and music shops and bookstores were commonplace.

When my legs became tired from walking, I stopped in at a café and ordered a latte and a caramel slice. I sat down in an armchair and looked out the window. I realised I could see myself living here, enjoying the culture and the atmosphere.

Perhaps law school is my future after all?

A young man sat across from me in the café, doodling in a sketchbook. My thoughts immediately turned to Julian. I instinctively checked my phone.

One new message. My heart thudded.

Good. Let me know how you get on tomorrow. Mum had responded to my text message from earlier.

I deflated.

After I finished my coffee, I made my way back to the hotel. Fortunately, I had been careful to keep track of where I went. The town was a bit like a maze.

Back in the hotel, I lazed around, flicking through the TV channels. I ordered dinner through room service. That made me feel so fancy and grown up. I hoped my parents wouldn't mind the bill.

My phone vibrated on the bedside table.

Hope you're having a good time in Wellington. J.

I held the phone to my chest, overjoyed Julian had texted me. When I had recovered from my moment of jubilation, I replied.

I am. But it's strange to think I will live here next year.

Julian texted back. *It suits you. Let me know how the open day goes.*

I smiled and typed my reply. *I will.*

Goodnight.

I sighed deeply, turning onto my stomach.

I awoke disorientated, which usually happens when I don't spend the night in my own bed. The alarm clock read 9:12.

Shit.

I must have forgot to set the alarm. I got dressed in a hurry and flung my bag over my shoulder. The walk to the university was a long and arduous journey by foot. When the campus finally came into view, I was exhausted. A sprawl of large, intimidating buildings surrounded me. I entered a courtyard and followed the sound of chatter. A group of nervous young people stood outside.

I'm in the right place.

After a few minutes of standing around, a stern-looking old man let us into a lecture theatre. I sat at the front and took out my notepad and pen.

The old man stood at the lectern. "Quiet please," he said, but the noise didn't die down. He raised his voice. "Quiet."

That did the trick.

He cleared his throat. "Welcome prospective law students." He started a slide deck projected on the wall. "Hill University is the first and foremost place to study law in New Zealand. Our programme is unrivalled. We have access to the country's largest library of legislation. Parliament and the supreme court are on our doorstep. Past students have gone on to become some of the world's top lawyers." He went through the slides, sharing some of the key benefits of studying law at the university.

The excitement of the students around me was palpable, but my mind wandered while the old man droned on in monotone.

After the presentation, we were put into small groups, each led by a student representative from the university. Each group set off in different directions for a tour of the campus and the Law School facilities. The campus was quiet, with only a few students about, as it was semester break. We came to the main law building, tall and foreboding.

"This is one of the oldest buildings in the university," the student rep explained. She opened the door and took us inside.

The interior was overwhelmingly brown, and a musty smell pervaded the air. Wooden desks and blackboards in the classrooms made me feel like I had stepped back in time. Next, we were taken to the library. The huge, multi-floored room housed shelves packed with thick volumes of legislation. When I removed a dense hardcover, a cloud of dust filled the air and I sneezed. I flicked through the first few pages before my arms grew tired from its heft.

When the tour came to an end, I went outside and gasped in the fresh air. I checked the time. One o'clock. Still plenty of time before I had to make it to the airport. I left the campus to explore the area a bit more. After an extensive walk around, I managed to wind up in a seedy part of town, full of sex shops and massage parlours. But cafés, bookshops and theatres also featured in the eclectic mix of businesses.

Down a back road, a brick building caught my eye. *Elias Institute* the sign read above the entrance. The name rang a bell. I recalled seeing their stall at the careers fair. I wondered whether it might be possible to go in and take a look around.

I crossed the road and stood at the entrance. The door was locked. An access card was required to get in.

Well, that is that, then.

I turned around and saw two people—a young man and a woman—heading towards the building. The man took out an access card, and they went in.

Now's my chance. I swooped in behind them. *I'm in.*

The foyer was a large and airy atrium, with a beautiful mosaic floor polished to a gleam and a trickling fountain.

Wow. I stood there stunned. *What a beautiful school…*

After I had finished staring in awe, I ascended the staircase to the next level. The floor housed several small classrooms and cute little studios. I took my time wandering around, admiring each room. I couldn't help but fantasise about studying here. Caught up in my thoughts, I managed to walk straight into someone.

"Hey, watch where you're going," the man from earlier said, with the woman still by his side.

"Uh…I'm sorry."

The pair scrutinised me through narrowed eyes.

"What are you doing here? You're not a student, are you?" the man asked.

I tried to act casual. "I'm just a visitor. Are you students here?"

"Yup," the woman said. "We're second-year students. I'm Amy, and this is Mark."

"I'm Ivy. So, what do you guys study?"

"Mark studies photography, and I study creative writing."

My pulse sped up. *Creative writing.* "Cool! I'd love to study creative writing here…"

"We can give you a tour if you like."

Mark checked his watch. "I don't have long."

"It will be a whirlwind tour, then."

"That's fine. Thanks!" I said, eager for the opportunity to explore the school.

Mark and Amy showed me around the rest of the floor.

"The classrooms here are so small," I remarked.

"Uh huh," Amy said. "It's better that way. Everyone can get attention from the tutor."

We turned a corridor, and Mark showed us into one of the art studios.

"There are facilities here for everything," Mark explained. "Painting, sculpting, photography, you name it."

I gaped at the spacious room, lined with workbenches and stools. Shelving overflowed with an endless variety of tools and materials.

I lagged behind when Amy and Mark continued to the stairs.

"Up here is the library and study area," Amy said as we ascended.

I quickened my pace, eager to see the room ahead. My heart fluttered at the sight of the beautifully furnished library with good condition books in perfect alignment on the shelves.

When I found the effort to tear myself away, up we went to the next floor. We entered a narrow corridor with many doors lining the sides. "Offices?" I asked.

Mark shook his head. "These are actually study rooms, or 'pods' as we call them."

"Every writing student gets their own pod assigned to them," Amy said. "It's the perfect, quiet space for writing." She led us farther down the corridor and opened a door. "This is my pod."

I immediately saw why it was referred to as a pod. The room was tiny, fitting only a small desk and a chair. Nevertheless, it seemed cozy and peaceful. And, most importantly, completely private.

"There's also a kitchen on this level. Good if you're planning on spending a long time here," Amy said.

We approached the stairs. "How many more levels?" I asked.

"This is the last one," Mark said.

"Offices," I declared again when we reached the landing.

"Yeah, you can visit your tutor here during their office hours."

Another staircase, leading up. "I thought we were at the top?"

Amy smiled. "Not quite."

On the next floor, she opened a door which led out onto the rooftop. The cool air rushed over me. The sunlight made me blink. When I had properly regained my vision, I took in the incredible view.

"Wow, you can see the whole city from up here."

"Pretty amazing, isn't it?" Amy stood beside me. "This is where the art students can paint or draw in the open air. Or you can just go to relax and get some fresh air."

I couldn't help thinking this school was a complete and utter dream. Turning to Mark and Amy, I expressed my gratitude. "Thanks for the tour. This seems like a wonderful place to study."

"Are you thinking of applying?" Amy asked.

"I'm not sure yet," I said, knowing all the while the sheer unlikelihood that would ever happen. Sighing, I checked my watch. "Is that the time? I need to get going."

"It was nice to meet you. If you come here next year, come say hi," Amy said.

"I will. Thanks again." I left the building in a hurry. I practically skipped down the road, my heart feeling like it was about to burst. Even though I knew I wouldn't get to go there, I couldn't help imagining what it would be like. I allowed a tiny sliver of hope to enter my thoughts.

12

I arrived home safe and sound on Sunday evening. Of course, Mum was dying to ask a million questions. I faked enthusiasm, while the Elias Institute occupied my mind. I didn't dare say anything, though. I held it all in until I had the chance to talk to Lana.

When I saw her the next morning, it all came tumbling out in a deluge. "It was like a dream, Lana. I never imagined a place like it."

"Sounds as if you're having second thoughts about Hill."

"I can't even think about Hill right now."

"What are you going to do?"

"I don't know, but I want to find out more about the Elias Institute."

"Why don't you ask the careers adviser?"

I nodded. "Good idea."

I headed to the careers office at lunch time. The tiny room occupied the top of B block. I realised I had never been in there before. I only knew where it was because my maths classroom was opposite to it. The door to the room stood ajar, so I walked in. A woman sat at the computer. She was old with greying hair tied back in a severe bun.

She looked up at me when I entered, and I assumed she must be the careers adviser. I had never seen her before. Most students probably hadn't, apart from those who had had their mandatory appointment with her in their final year. I hadn't had mine yet. I didn't even know her name.

The woman looked confused. "Do you have an appointment?"

"No. Is that okay? Do I need an appointment?"

"No. That's fine. What can I help you with?"

"Do you have any information on the Elias Institute?"

"I believe I do have that somewhere." She got down on her knees and scanned the lower shelves. "Ah. Here we go." She plucked a slim booklet from the bottom shelf. "This is the prospectus, and there's an application form inside."

"Thanks."

"What are you interested in studying?"

"Creative writing."

"Well, the Elias Institute certainly has a great offering in that regard. It is the only place in New Zealand to offer a Bachelor of Fine Arts with a creative writing major."

"Is that so? I just visited the campus last weekend. It was totally amazing."

"Elias is an elite school. I should warn you its courses are very difficult to get into. Not to mention, the fees are through the roof. It's a private school, you see."

"I didn't know that."

"It's something to keep in mind."

"Thanks for letting me know."

"Do you need anything else?"

I shook my head. "This will do for now." It's not as if I

actually planned on applying. Sheer curiosity had brought me here.

When I arrived home from school, I was eager to read the Elias prospectus.

"Good afternoon," Mum said as I entered the house.

"Home already?" I asked.

"Yes. I had an appointment this afternoon, so I left work early."

We briefly conversed before I slipped off to my room and shut the door firmly behind me. I lay on my bed and read through the prospectus cover to cover. The creative writing course sounded absolutely amazing. The course was purely dedicated to writing with a little reading sprinkled in for good measure. Workshops taught every aspect of story—plot, characters, language, themes and more. The course reading lists were comprised of the classics, and the tutors were all published authors.

Every student was encouraged to submit their manuscripts for publication at the end of the year. My palms grew sweaty as I turned each page. My heart raced. I knew this was it—the course my heart desired. Law school was nothing compared to this.

I allowed my mind to wander to thoughts of student life at Elias. Then I snapped out of it. My parents would never let me do this. End of story. My heart slowly sank in my chest.

"Ivy?" Mum began to open the door.

I jumped up and stuffed the prospectus under my mattress before she could see anything.

"Would you like something to eat? I bought scones from the bakery."

"Uh…sure." I didn't want to raise further suspicion, so I went to have afternoon tea with her.

"Are you all right? You're acting jumpy," Mum said.

"I am?"

"Is there something on your mind?"

I shook my head. I didn't dare tell her I was having second thoughts about studying law.

13

Julian texted me to arrange another modelling session. When I arrived, I was shocked by the state of disarray in his studio. The floor was covered in discarded pieces of paper, his tools were scattered, and his desk was piled up.

"What happened?" I asked, looking around.

Julian scratched his head. "Oh, sorry about that. I've let things get out of control. It's all because of something my teacher said."

"Sounds serious. Want to talk about it?"

Julian paced the room, arms crossed. "He gave me a pretty harsh critique. Said my work was too 'perfect' and it didn't have any energy."

"Too perfect? How can something be too perfect?"

"That's what I thought too. But in the back of my mind, I knew he had a point."

I remembered Woody Anderson's artwork at the exhibition, bold and bizarre. The complete opposite of Julian's style. It wasn't to my taste, but even I could tell it was on a different level to Julian's work. That's why he was a successful artist and Julian wasn't. At least, not yet. "Maybe you just need more practice?" I offered.

"I hope that's all it is. Woody has set me an exercise to help me 'loosen up.' Ten five-minute sketches. That's why I asked you here today."

"Okay. Where do you want me?"

Julian rubbed his chin in thought. "Let's start off with a standing pose. Lean with your back against the wall. Like this." He positioned me, gently pushing my shoulders back to the wall.

His touch made my skin prick, and our eyes briefly met. Heat rose to my cheeks. I flinched and broke eye contact. Julian stood back, gently biting his lip as he surveyed me. He repositioned my arm.

"There. That looks great." He pulled up a chair and, with his sketchpad resting on his knee, he began to draw me with brisk strokes.

When the five minutes were up, the timer on Julian's cell phone beeped. "Time for the next pose. Hmmm… Why don't you sit down at the desk?"

He cleared his desk by sweeping away the clutter onto the floor. He pulled out the chair for me and I sat down.

"That looks good," he said, surveying the scene.

I stared out the window while Julian drew me.

After five sketches were complete, a knock interrupted us. Priscilla came in holding a tray with pastries and a pot of tea.

"I thought you two could use a break. You've been working so hard."

Julian cleared a space on the floor and put some cushions down. We sat down together. Priscilla poured the cups of tea.

"Ivy, my dear, what's new in your world?"

My recent trip immediately sprang to mind. "I was in

Wellington last weekend. I went to the Law School open day at Hill."

"That's right," Julian said. "How was it?"

"Hill University was uninspiring, to say the least."

He scoffed. "No surprises there."

"But I was also able to visit the Elias Institute. Have you heard of it?"

"It was one of the places I thought about studying visual art. Oh, yeah. They do a creative writing major too, don't they?"

I nodded. "The campus is absolutely stunning. There are private study rooms for everyone. The tutors are all so accomplished..."

Julian smirked. "You sound excited just talking about it."

"I think it's my dream school. Too bad it's out of the question."

"Why is that?" Priscilla frowned.

"My parents want me to study law. They're going to pay for university and everything."

"But what do you want?"

I want to please my parents, but I also want to follow my dreams. Too bad it wouldn't be possible to do both.

"I don't know what I want."

"I'm sure you'll figure it out."

"I hope so."

"Just remember it's your decision. No one can make you do anything."

"I know." *Easier said than done.*

Our conversation turned to more light-hearted matters as we finished our tea.

When we were done, Priscilla left us to continue where we'd left off.

Julian began the next sketch, pencil in hand. I was posed on the couch, knees up and leaning against the arm.

I noticed, as time went on, Julian's strokes grew stiffer. He seemed tense. I could sense his growing frustration.

"Maybe we should stop here?" I suggested.

"No," Julian snapped.

I was taken aback by his abruptness. "Is everything okay?"

"Yes. Let's keep going."

"All right, then." I eased back into position.

Julian continued the sketch, but I could tell he wasn't into it. When his pencil lead snapped, he cursed and threw the pencil across the room.

"Julian—"

"I'm sorry. Let's stop."

"I thought this exercise was supposed to help you loosen up?"

"I'm not very good at that, am I?"

"You're just not in the right frame of mind tonight. We could try it another day."

"Thanks, but I'm not sure that will help." Julian's face blazed red.

I felt terrible for him. I wanted to comfort him so badly. "You'll make a breakthrough soon. I'm sure of it."

He exhaled deeply. "Yeah. I hope so." Doubt permeated his voice.

"Julian…?"

"Yes?"

Before I could fully think the implications through, I put my arms around him, drawing him into a hug. I sensed his bewilderment, his rigid body in my arms. I continued to hold him until his breathing calmed. Tentatively, he lifted his arm and returned the hug.

"What's this for?" he asked.

Embarrassment caught up with me, and I broke away. "You looked like you needed a hug."

Julian's eyes searched me, and I blushed.

A hint of amusement crossed his face. "I did. I feel much better now."

"Good."

Julian sighed and began to pace. "I think I'm just nervous."

"About what?"

"About Florence. About everything."

"Don't be nervous. This is what you've been working towards. You will finally achieve your dream. It's wonderful."

Julian stopped. "I know. I'm over-thinking things. Sorry."

"It's okay."

"Let's call it a night."

I nodded.

"Can I give you a ride?"

"Better not. My parents weren't too thrilled last time. I'll take the bus."

"Are you sure? Then let me walk you to the bus stop. It's dark out."

"Okay. Thanks."

Back downstairs, the lights had been turned off. Priscilla must have already left. Julian locked up. Outside, the air was crisp. We walked side by side down the road.

"This is it," I said when the bus stop came into view.

"I'll wait with you until the bus gets here."

"Thanks." I smiled appreciatively.

We didn't have to wait too long. The bus rumbled down the street. I signalled, and it pulled over.

"Goodnight, Julian."

"Goodnight." He waited as I got on the bus.

Taking my seat, I watched through the window as he walked off into the night.

Seeing Julian struggle with his art made me more determined than ever to practice my writing. Head down and blank notebook in front of me, I put pen to paper. I blocked out all negative thoughts and began to write. The words didn't flow at all, but I forced myself to continue. I filled one page, then one more, and then the next. After five pages, I stopped and read through what I had written. My heart sank.

This is complete and utter crap. I felt like tearing out the pages and starting over. *This must be how Julian felt*. I took a deep breath. *No. I won't give in to self-doubt*. With its pages still intact, I put the exercise book away.

On my way out of the library, I instinctively looked for Anna at the issues desk. In her place stood an old lady with long, silver hair and tiny, round spectacles.

I wonder how Anna's getting on. Her baby must be due around now. She could even be in hospital this very moment. I hoped she was okay.

I walked home from school. My over-enthusiastic mother arrived later in the evening.

"I have wonderful news, my darling," she said.

"What is it?"

"Work experience."

"What?"

"It's all arranged. Natalie Turner has agreed you can work at the firm over the holidays."

I groaned internally. I had forgotten all about this. Or,

perhaps, I had assumed it would just go away. I didn't know what to say. Mum was so happy.

"That's great, Mum," I said. If it didn't seem genuine, she didn't notice.

"Starting Monday, you're due in the office with me at 8:30 am every morning."

I physically recoiled.

"Don't look so shocked. It will be a worthwhile use of your holidays. This is real world experience to include on your CV and university application."

"I know, Mum."

She squeezed my shoulder. "This is just what you need. You'll see."

14

I woke to a blaring alarm. Wiping the sleep from my eyes, I reached out and turned it off. I couldn't believe it. The rest of my classmates would be sleeping in right now, and here I was, getting up even earlier than usual to go to work. I took a lukewarm shower to wake me up, then I got dressed. Although I had a lot of clothes, I didn't really have anything that looked professional. The best I could do was a dress and a cardigan. In the kitchen, Mum prepared breakfast. I sat at the dining table.

"Isn't this exciting?" Mum said as she spread jam on toast. "This is going to look amazing on your application to law school. How could they even think about turning you down now?"

I tried to take slow, deep breaths and calm myself down.

Just after eight, I bundled myself into the car with Mum. I had never been to Turner-Blomquist & Associates before, but I knew it was located in the only high-rise building in town. We took the lift up to the fifth floor and arrived at the reception, where I had to sign in on a guest book.

"Now, we're going to see Natalie," Mum said. "Don't be scared of her. She's not that bad."

I didn't think I would be scared, but now Mum had warned me, I wondered if I should be.

Down a long corridor, we reached an office at the back of the building. A name card on the door read, *N. Turner LLB (hons), LLM, MPhil*.

"Ready?" Mum asked.

I nodded meekly. She opened the door. We arrived in a sort of waiting room. A second door passed through to the inner sanctum. We crossed the divide and Mum gave a polite knock on the door before we entered.

Natalie sat at a grand mahogany desk. She was a blonde woman, middle aged—but who obviously took good care of her appearance. She strummed her perfectly manicured nails on the desk. Mum nudged me forward.

So, she isn't going to speak on my behalf, I realised.

I was terrified. "Uh, excuse me," I asked.

Natalie didn't look up from the paperwork preoccupying her.

"Excuse me, Ms. Turner," I said again.

Natalie looked up and narrowed her eyes. "For Heaven's sake, speak up."

"Ms. Turner," I began, raising my voice considerably. "I'm Ivy Beckett. I'm here for work experience."

"Work experience?" She consulted the large diary on her desk. "Very well." She looked at Mum. "Karen, show her around and introduce her to everyone."

Mum nodded.

"Then, Ivy, report back here to me."

I almost instinctively said "Yes, sir" but stopped myself just in time.

Mum took me around the floor. It felt like a maze with twisting corridors and door after door. She showed me where the bathroom and kitchen were first. Then she took me around the various offices, except for any which were occupied by clients. Most of the people I met seemed grumpy and not too pleased to see me.

After Mum finished giving me the tour, she reassured me, "You'll be fine. I'll be in my office, just next door to Natalie's, if you need me."

Back at Natalie's office, she had me sit at the desk in the waiting room.

"You are to greet anyone who comes in and fetch them a glass of water, tea or coffee if they want one. Ring me if anyone is waiting. You are to answer the phone when it rings. Do not put any calls through to me. I'm busy. Take a message instead and write it down in the notebook on the desk."

Nervousness rippled through my stomach. What if I took a message down incorrectly? What if I got peoples' names wrong? I just had to force it out of my mind and focus on surviving one day at a time.

I sat at the desk, and Natalie went back into her office and closed the door firmly behind her. For a while, I just sat there aimlessly. The phone didn't ring, and no one arrived to see Natalie. After a while, I decided it wouldn't hurt if I did a bit of writing during my downtime. I had brought a notebook with me. As time went by, I decided the job wasn't so bad after all.

I was startled when Natalie came out of her office.

"Can you do a coffee order?" she asked.

Before I could respond, she began rattling off a list of coffees. I grabbed a pen and wrote them down. I didn't dare ask her to repeat the order, so I hoped I had it down right.

"We have an account at Antoine's. Just say bill it to Turner-Blomquist," Natalie explained.

"Right. Where is Antoine's?"

She sighed as if I should know exactly where it is.

"It's opposite the church. Across the courtyard."

"Oh. Okay," I said, although I didn't know where the church was.

Natalie left, and I tried to ask Mum, but she was on the phone.

I guess I'm on my own.

It felt nice to get some fresh air after being holed up all morning. Much to my relief, I managed to find the church, and after a thorough stroll around the courtyard, I saw the café. I placed the order at the counter and said to put it on the Turner-Blomquist account. I was mentally prepared to be questioned, but all went smoothly.

Juggling two cardboard cup holders in hand, I returned to Turner-Blomquist. Natalie wasn't in her office, and I had no idea where she went. I had to go ask Mum what to do.

"She's probably in the board room," Mum said.

"Is it okay if I just go in and give them the coffee?"

"Yes. Just don't draw too much attention to yourself."

I nodded and went to the board room. The doors were closed, but I didn't knock. I just slipped in with the coffee, placed it on the table and slipped out again. Natalie didn't so much as give me a glance of acknowledgement. When I got back to my desk, I had my first phone call.

"Turner-Blomquist, Natalie's office," I said, having first rehearsed what I'd say in my mind.

"Yes, is Natalie available please?"

"I'm sorry. She's in a meeting."

"Do you know when she'll be free?"

"No, sorry. Would you like to leave a message?"

"I'll just call back later."

"Okay."

"Thanks, bye."

"Bye."

I sighed, knowing full well that if he called back later he still wouldn't be able to talk to her. He should've just left a message.

By midday, I was beginning to get hungry. I wasn't quite sure when I should get up to have lunch. Should I let Natalie know? Should I eat at my desk or in the kitchen? Or could I go outside? There was so much I didn't know about workplace etiquette, and I supposed it also varied from workplace to workplace.

When my stomach began to growl loudly, I wandered to the kitchen. I took my lunch out of the fridge, microwaved it and ate in the kitchen. After filling the void in my stomach, I went back to my desk. The phone rang several more times in the afternoon.

Late in the afternoon, I was winding down and preparing to leave when the phone rang again.

"Hello," said a strange voice.

"Hi," I replied, a little taken aback.

"I want to speak to Mummy."

"Is your mum's name Natalie?"

The boy took a few seconds to respond.

"Yes."

"Okay, hold on. I'll tell her."

Natalie had told me not to put any calls through to her, but surely she would want to speak to her own son. I took a deep breath before knocking on Natalie's door.

"Yes?" Her voice was rife with irritation, and her eyes blazed.

I gulped. "Excuse me, Natalie, but your son is on the phone. He wants to speak to you."

"I'm busy."

"But—"

"Tell him I'll see him tonight."

"Oh. Okay."

I couldn't believe she would snub her own child like that. Having to let the little boy down upset me greatly.

"I'm sorry, your mum is busy. She will see you tonight."

"Okay." The boy sounded as if he were about to cry.

I wanted to say something to him, but it was too late. He hung up. The experience left a sour taste in my mouth. How could Natalie be so cold?

The clock ticked five o'clock, and I was desperate to get home. But I was afraid to just up and leave. Natalie was still in her office and probably would be until far later. I was sure Mum would come get me when it was time to go. Soon, it was ten past, and then twenty past. Finally, at twenty-five past Mum collected me. On our way out of the building, I saw most employees were still there, working.

Upon arriving home, I realised I had never been so exhausted.

So, this is what it's like to go to work? I had been so naïve. School was blissful compared to this.

After dinner, I took a long, relaxing bath. Then, it was time for a cup of tea and zoning out in front of the TV, which I almost never did. Tiredness set in early, and I went straight to bed. I fell asleep quickly.

~

When the weekend finally arrived, I thought it would be a welcome reprieve. But, much to my dismay, it came and went in a flash. On Sunday evening, I felt nauseous. Never had I so dreaded the arrival of Monday. I hoped working for real wouldn't feel this way.

When my alarm went off on Monday, I groaned. I almost fell immediately back to sleep, but the movement going on in the hallway kept me awake—barely. I dragged myself out of bed.

"You look pale," Mum said when I met her in the kitchen.

"I don't feel great." The dread of facing the week ahead made me feel sick.

"Well, perk up," Mum said without an ounce of sympathy.

I took a deep breath and tried to muster as much positivity as I could.

When we got to work, I went to the kitchen to put my lunch in the fridge. A man with a bristly moustache and red cheeks stood making a cup of tea.

"Hi, Jerry," I said, remembering his name.

"I'm sorry, what's your name again?"

"It's Ivy. I'm here on work experience."

"That's right, your Karen's daughter."

I nodded.

"How's it going so far?"

"It's okay. All I have to do is answer phone calls, take messages and get coffee or lunch for Natalie."

"Are you managing to stay on her good side?"

"I think so."

"Are you studying law next year?"

"I might be."

"It's a good career. But you need to love it. Otherwise, it'll slowly grind down your will to live."

That didn't reassure me one bit. "Uh, thanks for the advice."

Natalie had several clients lined up for meetings that day, so I was continually on my feet, making them tea or coffee and trying to give them the impression they were important to Natalie. I was well out of my comfort zone.

Whenever I had a free moment, I opened my notebook and escaped to my happy place—my creations; my stories. It gave me a sense of calm. Through the wall to Natalie's office, I heard her yelling hysterically over the phone to someone.

Why does Mum idolise her so much? As far as I was concerned, I would never want to end up like Natalie Turner. She was cold, mean and a workaholic. I envisaged a life for myself far different than this.

This is not the life I want, I thought bitterly.

I remembered Julian saying, *"You should do what you love."*

I still had the booklet for the Elias Institute safely tucked under my mattress, the application form enclosed within.

You don't need to do what your parents tell you. You can make your own decisions. Would it hurt just to apply and see what happens? Just thinking about the possibility of attending Elias instantly made me feel better. All my fear and worries slipped away. I would do it.

On Thursday, Natalie told me I was dismissed and could go home and enjoy the rest of the holidays. I honestly wasn't sure whether this was a reward for my hard work or a punishment for doing something wrong I wasn't aware of. Natalie had barely said a word to me, except to order me to do something. Mum thought she must have decided I'd done enough. I was working for free after all. I left early on Thursday, catching the bus home while Mum continued at work.

On Friday, Mum presented me with a typed recommendation signed by Natalie Turner. "This will practically confirm your place at law school."

I took the letter from her hand and read it through. *Exceptional young lady… Hardworking… Conscientious…*

"Did Natalie really write this?" I asked.

"It doesn't matter, does it? It has her signature on it."

"Did *you* write this?"

"Maybe. Who cares? This is all you need."

I sighed. I wondered whether Natalie had even bothered to read it. So many things must pass across her desk daily. Not that it mattered anyway. Words could not express my relief at being free from that dreary, soul-sucking place.

In the safety of my room, I fished out the Elias prospectus from under my mattress.

15

As soon as I walked onto the school grounds, Lana came at me with her arms wide open.

"I've missed you!" She drew me into a tight hug.

"Me too." I patted her on the back before gently peeling myself away. "What did you get up to over the holidays?"

"I was working a lot at the hospital. So, I spent most of my holidays pushing wheelchairs, cleaning up messes and talking to old people."

I wondered how she did it. She was a saint.

"My parents hired a tutor as well. When I wasn't at the hospital, I was revising for exams."

"So, you didn't have a break at all?"

"No. Not really."

"God, Lana, that's insane! How do you possibly manage?"

She shrugged. "It's fine. I'm used to it. Anyway, enough about me. How was Turner-Blomquist? I'm dying to know."

I took a deep breath.

"Not good?"

"Let's just say that working at Turner-Blomquist has put me off studying law once and for all."

Lana's eyes widened. "Wow. That's a big deal, Ivy."

"I know."

"What are you going to do?"

"I'm going to apply to the creative writing programme at the Elias Institute."

Lana yelped with joy. "That's amazing! It will be perfect for you."

"Yeah. I want this so much."

"It's good to know what you want."

"It feels like a huge relief."

"So..." Lana chewed her lip. "What do your parents think?"

I frowned. "They don't know yet."

"You'll have to tell them at some point."

"Yeah. I know."

The bell cut our conversation short.

"Let's talk more in English," Lana said.

We parted ways.

During form class, Lana's words circled my mind. *"You'll have to tell them at some point."*

I became all hot and nervous just thinking about it. No scenario I imagined had a happy ending. My parents would hate me for this, and I could kiss the money they had saved for me goodbye.

"Ivy, are you feeling okay?" Miss April asked, drawing the whole class's attention to me.

"I'm fine," I croaked.

"Your face is all red."

Even more heat spread across my face. "I'm just a little hot."

"Okay. If you don't feel well, please visit the sick bay."

"I'm fine, really." I sunk down in my seat, embarrassed.

The cool air soothed my hot face when I left the classroom. My temperature came down, and I could think clearer. I walked across the courtyard to B block. Lana was already seated in English class.

"So, when's the application to Elias due?" she asked before my butt even hit the chair.

"Early September. I need to check the exact date again."

"Will you bring it up with your parents before then?"

I tensed up. "I'll try to."

Mr. Donaldson arrived, but we continued our conversation via notes scrawled on a blank page of my exercise book.

You should tell them soon.

I'm scared!

Best get it over with.

I know .

Lana was right. The only way to put my mind at ease was to tell them. I would feel much better when it was all out in the open.

Later in class, I felt my phone vibrate in my skirt pocket. When Mr. Donaldson wasn't looking, I took it out and checked to see a message from Anna.

Oh? What's this?

I opened the message, and a picture slowly loaded. When the image was revealed, I instantly forgot all my worries. My heart flooded with joy at the sight of a tiny, adorable baby.

Lana must have noticed my sudden change in temperament. She grabbed the phone. Her eyes scanned the screen and she let out an audible squeal.

Mr. Donaldson cleared his throat. "Settle down girls. I know English is exciting, but please try to contain yourselves."

Blushing, I put my phone away. I'd think about contacting Anna later. For now, my first mission was to complete my application to Elias, plus the dreaded task of telling my parents.

That evening, I pulled out the Elias prospectus once again. If I was serious about applying, I shouldn't hesitate any longer. The prospectus was battered and dog-eared from the many times I had read it through. Inside, it was full of sticky notes and highlights.

I flipped to the back, found the application form and lifted it out. Holding it in my sweaty hands, I read through the requirements. Applicants had to have achieved university entrance to be eligible. A major must be selected—visual art, film and media or creative writing. A portfolio of work must be submitted, as well as a personal statement, CV, letters of recommendation, and transcripts of academic results.

The portfolio for the creative writing programme had to consist of two or more pieces of writing, totalling approximately five-thousand words. I reminded myself I had the short story I wrote for English up my sleeve, but I would still need to write something else as well to reach the word requirement. I sighed, thinking of the work ahead of me. Luckily, there was still plenty of time left before the application needed to be sent in. I was sure to come up with an idea before then.

While I continued to pour over the application form, my door opened. I leapt out of my chair, bewildered. Dad quirked an eyebrow at my flustered state.

He held the phone in his hand. "My mum is on the phone. She'd love to talk to you."

"You scared me," I said, catching my breath.

"Sorry." He didn't appear to notice the form on my desk. "I'll leave you to talk in peace." He handed me the phone and quietly exited.

"Grandma?" I asked, holding the phone to my ear.

"Oh, Ivy, darling! I'm so glad to hear your voice."

"Me too. It's been a while since we last talked."

"Too long."

"I'm sorry I haven't called you lately."

"That's fine, dear. I know you're a busy young woman. How are things? How's school?"

"School is fine. Preparation for exams hasn't really begun yet. We're still finishing off internal assessments."

"Getting good marks?"

"Yes, Grandma."

"That's my girl."

"How's everything at the lodge?"

"Business has been booming. Your grandpa and I are actually feeling a little overwhelmed. We're not going to take so many bookings after the rush has died down. We want a bit of a break."

"That's a good idea. You shouldn't overdo it."

"We won't. Now, listen, we haven't seen you in a while. Whenever will you visit?"

"Mum and Dad have been so busy with work. They haven't had much time—"

"I'm talking about *you*, dear. Why don't you come down to visit? You, by yourself. Or with a friend."

"Really?"

"Yes. We'll make sure there's a nice room available for you. We'd love to see you again. How long has it been, three or four years?"

"Has it really been that long?"

"Yes, I think so."

"Okay. I would love to visit. Can I really bring a friend?"

"Absolutely. You just call me when you've decided when to come down. I'll sort everything out for you. We'd love to have you here."

"Okay. I just need to work it out with school and everything."

"I understand. The lodge has changed a lot since you were last here."

"I can't wait to see it."

"You'll love it! I've missed you so much, Ivy. We, your grandpa and I, both have."

"I've missed you too."

"Okay, well, I suppose I'd better leave you to the rest of your evening."

"Okay, Grandma. Talk to you soon."

"Bye. Oh, Grandpa says hi!"

"Say hi back to him for me. Bye."

I loved it down at the lodge. According to my Dad, it had expanded a lot in recent years and had become quite famous. Many celebrities had stayed there, but my grandparents wouldn't say who. They respected their guests' privacy.

I returned to my desk. As I filled out my application, I started making plans in my head for a trip to the lodge.

16

Two weeks after the birth of Anna's child, I decided to pay her a visit. Carrying flowers and a soft toy, I approached Anna's house in the Knightsgate subdivision. The houses were all large and modern, with tiny, well-manicured gardens out front. The streets were quiet, apart from the distant hum of a lawnmower. I stood on the front step of Anna's house and knocked on the door.

A few moments later, Anna's husband, Paul, greeted me. "Hi, Ivy. Nice to see you." He was unshaven and had dark rings below his eyes.

"These are for you and Anna, and the baby," I said, handing over the flowers and toy.

"Thank you, Ivy. That's very kind." He added them to a pile of gifts accumulating on the hallway sideboard.

"How's Anna? Is she up to seeing anyone?"

"She's very tired."

"Oh, that's fine. I just came to drop these off."

"Thanks, Anna will be very happy."

"I hope you're both coping okay with everything."

Paul nodded. "It's been an eye-opening experience, but so far so good."

"Keep me in mind as a future babysitter."

He laughed. "Will do."

I was about to leave when Anna peeped her head around the corner. She was in a dressing gown and slippers. Her hair was a mess, but despite that, she seemed cheerful.

"Ivy!"

"Hey," I said.

"Simon has just nodded off."

"You can get some rest."

Anna nodded. "For a little while, at least."

"I'll leave you to it."

"Ivy, before you go, I have something to say."

"What is it?"

"I have news about Alexander Morris."

"You do? Can you tell me?"

"Not right now. I'm too exhausted to think straight. Let's meet up soon, though. My parents are coming up next week to help out. That will give me a bit of a break."

"Cool. Catch you next week. Can't wait to hear the latest news."

Anna beamed. "There's so much to tell you."

I arranged to meet Anna at a small coffee shop near her house. She was already there when I arrived, nursing a mug of hot chocolate. I ordered the same and sat opposite her.

"How's Simon doing?" I asked.

"He's doing just fine. He's a sweet little baby. When he's not crying and screaming his head off, that is."

"Is he sleeping?"

"Sporadically."

"At least you have your parents to help now."

"It's such a relief they're here." She exhaled audibly.

"I'm sure it's nice to have their support."

"Yeah. Otherwise, I'd be completely overwhelmed. I knew it would be hard, but it's so much harder than I ever imagined."

I couldn't even comprehend the work involved in looking after a newborn baby, but somehow, I empathised with her. "If there's anything I can ever do to help, just let me know."

Anna smiled. "You're very sweet, Ivy."

I shrugged shyly.

"Enough baby business. Let's talk about Alexander Morris."

My mind switched to the task at hand. "What did you find out?"

Anna reached into her handbag and pulled out a paperback called *The Drifting Girl*. "It arrived a few weeks ago." She passed it to me.

The book was weightier than *Hole Hearted*, and the glossy cover depicted a vacant-eyed girl's reflection in rippling water. I opened the book to a random page and read a passage.

> *The room had been preserved in the exact condition as she had left it. Boy band posters on the wall, bed unmade, laundry on the floor. I smoothed the bed cover and felt a pang of guilt. What am I doing here?*

Those words were familiar. "It's the same as *Hole Hearted*," I concluded.

Anna nodded. "It's in the small print." She took the book

and turned to the front matter. She ran her finger down the page. "Here it is. 'First published in New Zealand as *Hole Hearted*, 1995.'"

"So, it's true. Mr. Donaldson is Alexander Morris…"

Anna nodded. "I've reread it too. It's largely the same, but I did notice a few differences. Some parts are more graphic, more visceral."

"Interesting. Maybe the other publisher had wanted him to tone it down?"

"That's what I was thinking."

I took a long sip of hot chocolate while my brain processed everything. "I wonder why Mr. Donaldson keeps his pen name a secret?"

"Alfred is the only person who can answer that. Maybe he'd be willing to talk about it if you ask."

Ask Mr. Donaldson? I couldn't fathom bringing up something so private. Yet, I was beyond curious. What would it hurt?

"You're right. I'll ask him."

"To be honest, I'm dying to know as well. Let me know what he says."

"I will." I had something else I wanted to ask him as well.

Plucking up my courage, I visited Mr. Donaldson after school the next day. He sat at the desk in his office, hunched over slightly and attending to a stack of marking. He looked up and peered at me through his glasses.

"Ivy, what brings you here? It's home time."

I approached him, pulling up a chair. "I tried to catch you earlier, but you seemed busy."

He put down his pen. "What's on your mind?"

"I wanted to let you know I've decided to apply for a creative writing course after all."

"Is that so?" The corners of his eyes crinkled as he smiled. "That's simply wonderful. Which course have you decided on?"

"A Bachelor of Fine Arts at the Elias Institute, majoring in creative writing."

"That sounds ideal. Good on you."

"I need to submit a portfolio of my writing. Do you have any advice? What kind of thing might they be looking for?"

Mr. Donaldson scratched his chin. "Let's see now. Have you been writing every day?"

"Yes."

"Then you should be in good shape. Why don't you let me have a look over what you've been working on?"

"No," I spluttered, horrified. "It's all terrible."

He laughed. "Is that so?"

"None of that stuff is good enough for a portfolio."

"Of course, it's not. That's what editing is for. I would encourage you to read over all you've done. You're bound to come across something that has potential. Rewrite it, polish it, then send it my way. I will give you some pointers."

I was nervous about him reading my work, but a critique from Mr. Donaldson would surely prove beneficial. "Thanks. That would be a big help."

"Was there anything else?"

"Yes, actually." I suddenly grew embarrassed. There could be a good reason why Mr. Donaldson kept his pen name a secret. "I was wondering about Alexander Morris."

"Alexander Morris," Mr. Donaldson repeated, a twinkle in

his eye. "So, you know about Alexander Morris? You continue to surprise me."

I was taken aback by his reaction. He didn't seem to mind at all.

"However, did you find out about that?"

"It was Anna, the librarian. She worked it out."

"Anna?" Mr. Donaldson smiled. "Why does that not surprise me? I used to be her teacher too, not so long ago."

"You were Anna's English teacher?" I knew Anna had gone to this school, but somehow, I had never considered we might have shared the same teacher.

"Yes. Come to think of it, you and Anna are a lot alike."

I thought of Anna, smiling warmly from behind the issues desk, a book in her hand. "Really?" I asked.

He nodded. "She was the top student in her year. As I'm sure you can imagine, there were a lot of expectations placed on her. She was told she could succeed at anything."

"What happened?"

"One day, she confided in me that the only thing she wanted to do with her life was read. How she despaired of that." He chuckled.

I sighed, resting my head in my hand. "I know that feeling."

"It seems like everything worked out for her in the end."

"She loves being a librarian."

"I'm glad. I seem to have gotten off track. What were we talking about?"

"Alexander Morris."

"That's right. What did you wish to know about Alexander Morris?"

"I want to know why you don't tell anyone about him."

"Have you read any of his books?"

I shook my head. "Only *Hole Hearted*."

"The content can be challenging at times. Disturbing, even. You might say Alexander Morris is my dark side."

"But you're such a good writer. Surely, it deserves to be known?"

"First and foremost, I'm a teacher. I wanted to keep my writer side and my teacher side as separate as possible."

"So, it's to protect your job?"

"Originally, yes."

"But not anymore?"

"I'm an old man, Ivy. The funny thing about getting older is the things that once worried you no longer seem like a big deal. I wonder whether it's time?"

"Time for what?"

"Time to reveal the identity of Alexander Morris. What do you think?"

"Of course you should!"

Mr. Donaldson laughed. "Then I'll consider it."

"Anna will be ecstatic."

"Now, go on. Get yourself home."

I left his office and walked home in triumph. I couldn't wait to share the good news with Anna. Approaching my house, I noticed Mum's car parked in the driveway.

That's odd. She must have come home early. I could hear her in the kitchen. I went straight to my room. The moment I walked in, a sense of dread set in. Something was off. The bedding had been pulled from my bed, leaving a stark-naked mattress. The Elias prospectus which I kept hidden under my mattress jumped to my mind. I went to check that it was still there. I lifted the mattress and felt underneath.

Nothing.

17

I lifted the mattress farther to take a proper look. The Elias prospectus had vanished. I knew Mum must have taken it. I felt sick. Pacing my room, I wondered whether I should keep quiet or get it over with and confront her now. Either way, there was no way she would let this slip by.

I couldn't avoid Mum forever, so I crept to the kitchen under the guise of making a cup of tea. I tried to act all calm and cool.

Nothing out of the ordinary here. Then, I met her eyes, which were ablaze with simmering fury.

"I took your bedding to the dry cleaners," she said ominously.

I gulped. "Thanks."

"While I was taking off your mattress protector, I found something."

"Oh?"

"Don't play dumb." She picked up the prospectus from the coffee table. "What is this about, hmmm? Why were you hiding it?"

"I was just curious about what other options are out there. But, I thought you wouldn't approve."

"You're damn right I don't approve." She flicked through it, and the half-finished application form drifted to the floor.

I tried to grab it, but Mum was too fast.

"What's this? Application to study?" Her face twisted in disgust. "Didn't we agree you would study law?"

"I don't recall a formal and binding agreement."

"What's the issue here, Ivy? You've always had an interest in law. It's a good, sensible career choice."

"I *did* have an interest in it."

"And you still do, don't you?"

"Now, I'm not so sure. Maybe I was only interested in the first place because you pushed me so hard into it."

"I did no such thing."

I breathed in deeply, trying my best to stay calm. "I'm not cut out to be a lawyer. I want to do something creative."

"It's fine you're a creative person, Ivy. I encourage that. But creativity doesn't pay the bills."

"Lots of people manage to—"

"In this economy? I don't think so. How about your friend… What's his name? The artist boy."

"Julian?"

"That's right, Julian. How's it working for him? Got money to burn, has he?"

"No. But he hasn't even begun his study yet. He's still a novice."

Mum wasn't listening. "I know what it's like to struggle. Your dad was a journalist on minimum wage, and I was a post-grad student. We lived in poverty. I don't want that kind of life for you."

"It all worked out in the end though, didn't it?"

"Not without a lot of sacrifice. When we had you, I had to drop out of school, and your dad had to move into sales. If we could turn back the clock, we would have done things differently."

"What does that mean?" I asked, tears filling my eyes. *Is she referring to not having me? Was I a mistake?*

"I only want what's best for you."

"And how do you know what that is?" I spluttered through tears.

"I know I don't want you to go through the things your dad and I did."

"What was so bad?"

"I sacrificed my dreams to raise you."

"And, now, you want me to sacrifice mine?"

Mum opened her mouth to speak, but she couldn't find the words to retaliate.

I stormed off to my room and slammed the door behind me. I lay down, face buried in my pillow, muffling the sound of my crying. *Why won't she let me do what I want to do? Why does it hurt her so much?* I couldn't wrap my head around it. Exhausted and confused, I wept until my pillowcase was damp with tears. Sometime later, a faint knock caught my attention.

"Ivy? Can I come in?" Dad asked.

"No," I replied.

He opened the door anyway and sat down on the edge of my bed. "Ivy, I want to know what's going on."

"I don't want to talk about it." Tears welled in my eyes again.

"Please…why the sudden interest in another degree?" He patiently waited for me to recover from my crying.

"It's been on my mind for a while, but I knew Mum would

be pissed off about it," I sobbed.

"I thought you wanted to study law?"

"Mum wanted me to want to study law so bad she made me believe it. But I've snapped out of that, and I know it's not for me. I want to give writing a go. I know it's not a sensible career, but I'll never know if I can make it if I don't try."

Dad rubbed the bridge of his nose as he always did when deep in thought. He smiled.

"You know, I did the same thing at your age. I wasn't focused on a career. I just did what I wanted to do."

Sniffing back my tears, I sat up straighter, intrigued. "What did you do?"

"I played music with a band and I studied English at university."

"I didn't know you were a musician."

"Not a very good one. But I fancied the idea that I might become a music journalist."

"What happened?"

"It turned out to be much more difficult to get into than I expected. I wrote some articles for small publications. Most of the time, I didn't get paid anything. I wasn't able to get that big break I needed."

"When did you start working at the *Flagstaff*?"

"I bummed around for a while. Then when I needed to get serious about making money, I became a writer at the *Flagstaff*."

"So, that's when it happened..." I processed Dad's story in my mind. Still, something didn't make sense. "Why did you stop being a journalist? Did Mum make you give it up?"

Dad furrowed his brow. "Whatever gave you that idea?"

"You loved being a journalist, but you started working in sales around the time I was born."

"No one made me do anything. It's complicated."

"Tell me. I want to know."

Dad ran a hand through his hair and sighed. "All right, then. If you must know, so be it. But don't tell Karen I told you. She's very sensitive about this part of her life."

"I won't."

Dad made himself comfortable and then began. "I was working at the *Flagstaff,* and Karen was in her final year at university, completing a Masters in Law. I really wanted a baby."

"But not Mum?"

"She did, but she was very focused on her career at the time. She had this lofty idea of becoming a successful, high-profile lawyer."

"What changed her mind?"

"She agreed to have a baby if I would be a stay-at-home dad while she pursued her career. I was thrilled with the arrangement."

"But Mum ended up staying home…?"

"Yes, by a series of uncontrollable circumstances. She had a terrible pregnancy, you see. She was so ill, she stopped going to university. We planned that she would go back once you were born, but she was struck by postpartum depression."

No wonder Mum seems to resent me sometimes.

"By the time she had recovered, university had completely fallen from her radar. We desperately needed money. A job in advertising sales came up at the *Flagstaff,* and I decided to apply. It was a big increase in salary. I went to work, and Karen stayed home to look after you."

"So, that's how it happened," I said, downcast. All the jumbled pieces finally fit together. Mum had wanted to be a lawyer, but my birth had stopped her from achieving her goal. Now, she wanted me to pick up where she'd left off.

"I don't want you to think anything was your fault, Ivy. Sometimes dreams are just dreams and you have to let them go."

"But, still, you had the chance to try."

"I did, and I don't regret those days one bit. You would make a brilliant lawyer, Ivy. But I understand if your heart's not in it. It wouldn't be a good career if you hated it."

"I don't know if I would hate it. But I would regret not giving my writing a chance."

Dad nodded.

"So, what should I do?"

"You're adult enough to make your own decisions, whether your mum and I approve of them or not."

I nodded, although I desperately wanted approval—especially from Dad.

"We can't stop you from doing whatever you want. The worst we can do is hold back financial assistance, which I'm afraid will have to be the case. A university education is an investment, and creative writing is a risky path. I know that too well."

It hurt to hear it confirmed.

"I'll try to get your mother to calm down. It's best to avoid her for a while, though. Are you okay?"

"I'm okay."

Dad hugged me. "I love you."

"I love you too, Dad."

"Get some rest. I'll bring some food in for you later."

"Thanks."

Dad stood and left. The rest of the night, I stayed in my room, headphones on with loud music to try to drown out the sound of my parents arguing. Talking with Dad had made me feel better, but it didn't change the fact the Mum hated my guts, Dad wouldn't give me his blessing and I wouldn't get any money.

I slunk off to school the next day without so much as a word to my mother. I just couldn't face her. Nor could I face her after school. Instead of going home, I went straight to Opulence to see Priscilla. She would make me feel better.

When I entered the shop, Priscilla swept towards me. "Lovely to see you, Ivy."

"Thanks for letting me come over."

"Oh, that's fine. Is something bothering you?"

"I told my parents I want to study creative writing."

"Oh dear. And they didn't take it too well?"

"No. They didn't."

Priscilla hugged me. "Everything will be okay."

A customer entered the shop.

"Why don't you go make yourself comfortable upstairs? Julian's not here. I'll bring up tea later."

"Okay. Thanks."

I went upstairs while Priscilla attended to the customer.

The sunlight was already beginning to fade. I turned on the light in the studio. All was still. I looked at the easel to sneak a peek at Julian's work-in-progress—a picture of a beautiful girl sitting with a distant expression on her face. I admired the picture for a while before realising she looked familiar. Finally, it clicked.

It's me.

It was the finished version of the portrait he had been working on.

Is this how he sees me? I thought, somewhat surprised.

The more closely I looked at it, the more I could see the resemblance. I studied it for some time before going to Julian's desk. I pulled out my iPod and put my headphones on. While listening to music, I flicked through my notebook, cringing at the writing within.

Priscilla came up momentarily, carrying a silver tray. On it, were two teacups, a pot of earl grey and two slices of chocolate cake. "I've locked up downstairs."

"You didn't need to do that."

"I wanted to." She poured me a cup of tea. "Tell me everything."

I relayed everything to Priscilla while she listened attentively. When I had finished, Priscilla asked what I intended to do.

"I'm going to apply to the Elias Institute," I said, firmly.

"So, you're not going to back down?"

"No."

"And how do you feel about that?"

"Relieved, I guess."

"Then you know you've made the right decision."

"And my parents?"

"They'll get over it. If they love you, they'll understand."

I sighed. "It feels like my mum hates me right now."

"Just give her some time. She'll come around. I promise."

Talking with Priscilla made me feel much more at ease.

Heavy footsteps approached up the stairs. Julian entered. His hair was a mess, his eyes were red, and he hadn't shaved.

"You're back," Priscilla said.

"I left early. Ivy, what are you doing here?"

"Sorry, I was just..."

Julian grinned sheepishly. "Don't worry about it. You can come anytime you want." He sat down on the couch and yawned, stretching his arms above his head.

Priscilla checked the time. "I'm having guests over at my house tonight, so I'd better get going."

Julian nodded.

I started gathering my things.

Julian stopped me. "You can stay, if you want."

"Well, okay."

Priscilla left with a goodbye and a hug for each of us.

Before an awkward silence could pervade the room, I spoke. "I haven't heard from you in a while. Have you found a new model?"

"No. Actually, I haven't been drawing much lately. Not since the last time you came over."

"What? It's been a month!"

Julian hung his head. "I know."

"Are you still upset over what Woody said?"

"No. It's grown into something much bigger than that. I'm unable to work at all. I don't know what's happened to me."

So, a guy as talented as Julian could still suffer artist's block.

"Priscilla thinks I need a break."

"Sounds like a good idea."

Julian nodded. "I've pretty much been working non-stop since I left high school. That was more than two years ago now."

"No wonder you're burnt out."

"I'm thinking of going on holiday. Maybe a change of scenery will help me."

"Actually, I'm planning on taking a break myself."

"Really?"

"My grandparents own a lodge down south. They've invited me to come visit them."

"Sounds nice. I haven't been to the South Island in a long time."

I studied Julian's face. What would he say if I invited him? I was allowed to bring a friend with me, after all.

Before allowing myself to fully think it through, I blurted, "You know, they said it would be okay if I brought a friend along with me. You could come… If you want to."

Julian looked surprised, but not horrified by the suggestion, much to my relief.

"Really?"

"Yes. Lana can't come, so…"

"When do you plan on going?"

"Next weekend."

"That's soon. I can probably sort out someone to cover for me at Lucky Books…"

"So, you'll come, then?" I tried not to sound too delighted.

"Yes. If the offer's still available."

"Of course, it is. I'll tell my grandparents tonight. You'll need to sort your own plane ticket."

"That's fine."

"Great. Then it's agreed."

I kept waiting for Julian to change his mind, but he didn't. *This is really going to happen.* Julian and I would spend a weekend together. My mind raced with the possibilities. Julian seemed just as excited as me.

18

"Have a good time, my dear. Say hello to Ma and Pa for me," Dad said, passing me my bag from the boot.

"Will do." I gave him a hug goodbye and then entered the airport. After checking in, I looked around for Julian. I didn't see him anywhere. I checked my phone in case he had texted me.

No new messages.

I sat down in the departures area and pulled out one of the novels I had packed. I was deeply absorbed in the book when a hand touched my shoulder.

"Sorry I'm late," Julian said, his deep voice pulling me from the story. "I got stuck in traffic."

His chest quickly rose and fell. He must have rushed to get there in time. "It's okay." I glanced at the departures board. "The flight isn't boarding for a few more minutes."

Julian sat down beside me. "Hey, thanks for inviting me on this trip."

"It's no big deal. I prefer to go with someone anyway. The lodge is beautiful. I think the scenery will really inspire you."

"I don't want to get my hopes up, but I did bring supplies, just in case." He lifted a black portfolio case.

Our flight boarded shortly thereafter. As we traversed the windy tarmac, I wrapped my cardigan tighter around me.

Aboard the plane, Julian took my bag. "Let me help you with that." He put it in the overhead locker.

Although it had been a short time ago since I had last flown, I still felt nervous. I gripped the armrests tightly as the plane sped down the runway.

"Are you all right?" Julian asked.

"Yes," I squeaked.

When we were fully up in the air, I felt much more comfortable. Julian looked completely at ease, quietly reading a book. I supposed, with all the travel he'd done, he was used to it.

We hit a large bump midway through the flight. I yelped and clung to Julian's arm. Realising what I had done, I quickly let go. Julian smirked at me, amused. When we finally landed, I exhaled with relief.

My grandparents met us in the arrivals area. Grandma wore a floral dress, and Grandpa was wearing pants held up by suspenders, spectacles and a beret. They looked so sweet. They also looked much older than I remembered. It had been a few years after all. I rushed over to them. Julian lagged behind me.

"Ivy!" Grandma welcomed me with a warm embrace. She smelled like powder. "Look at you. My, how you've grown. And this handsome young fellow must be Julian."

"Nice to meet you." Julian kissed Grandma on the cheek and shook Grandpa's hand.

"How was the flight?" Grandpa asked as we made our way to the car.

"It was fine," I said.

"You were nervous," Julian chided.

"I wasn't."

"So, you grabbed hold of my arm for no reason?"

"No reason in particular."

"Aren't you two just adorable, quibbling like a married couple," Grandma said with a laugh.

We immediately ceased our argument, my face red.

The lodge was located forty minutes out from the airport. We drove several kilometres on winding country roads and hills. Eventually, we came to a signpost which read *Landsend Lodge,* with an arrow pointing up a steep road. We turned up the road and into the thick trees. After a few minutes, the trees cleared and we came to a black iron gate across the driveway that was closed.

Grandpa jumped out and typed in a passcode. The gate swung open, and we went up the drive. Julian and I gaped as the incredible grounds came into view. The beautiful gardens, tennis courts and pool made us too awestruck to speak. The main building loomed ahead, stately and classic.

"Here we are." Grandpa pulled up outside.

"This is amazing," I said, getting out of the car. "It's so different than the last time I came here."

"Impressed?"

"Very."

Grandma led the way to the entrance. "Come on in. Afternoon tea is waiting. Let's have a bite to eat and something to drink. Then, we'll give you the grand tour."

"Sounds great." I followed my grandparents into the building.

We entered a large reception room before being directed

down a long, wide corridor, and finally into a small parlour. An assortment of baked goods had been laid out on the table. Grandma brought in a fresh pot of tea.

"Looks delicious," I said. "You didn't need to go to so much trouble."

"Oh, it's no trouble at all, my dear," Grandma said.

I buttered a freshly-baked scone. "The lodge is so beautiful. Did you have a lot of work done?"

"We've had the house extended and refurbished. We've been so successful these last few years that expansion has been necessary," Grandpa said.

"I'm so happy for you."

"It's hard to believe this started out as a simple bed and breakfast. It has evolved a lot since then."

"Is there anyone staying here at the moment?"

"It's relatively quiet. But, yes, we have two couples staying."

When we had finished afternoon tea, my grandparents took us on a tour around the building.

"This is the indoor pool and relaxation area," Grandma said, showing us to a large, bright room with an immaculate, heated swimming pool. Windows looked out into the surrounding lush greenery.

I felt calm and relaxed simply upon entering the room. I couldn't wait to go for a swim and then relax in the spa pool. After a long period of marvelling at the pool, my grandparents ushered us away to see the restaurant. The small and intimate room housed just a few tables. Doors opened out onto a courtyard surrounded by gardens.

The next room of interest was the library. The floor-to-ceiling bookcases were well-stocked with fiction and nonfiction titles. A large fireplace dominated the centre of the back wall, and comfy armchairs surrounded a coffee table on a Persian rug.

"This is Heaven," I remarked.

Grandpa chuckled. "This room was my little project. I'm glad you like it."

We left the library and arrived where the hallway forked into two passages.

"The door on the right leads to our private wing, where your grandma and I live," Grandpa said. "To the left is the guest wing."

We walked down the guest wing. "Let's see your rooms," Grandma said, excitedly.

We stopped outside a door.

"Ivy, this is your room." Grandma opened the door to a large room with cream walls, a king-sized bed and a desk. The window had a gorgeous view of the lodge's grounds.

"It's perfect," I said.

"The bathroom is through here." Grandma opened a door.

The bathroom had a claw foot tub and a generous vanity stocked with fancy toiletries. The towels were large, white and fluffy.

Next, Grandma showed us Julian's room, which was opposite mine. It was similar, but he had a large drawing desk and a balcony on which a chair and easel were set up.

"Ivy told me all about your art," she explained. "I thought it would only be appropriate to have somewhere to work."

"Thanks. I'm sure I'll make good use out of it," Julian said.

Grandma looked pleased. "Right, I'll leave you two to it. Do go out and have a look around the grounds. Please meet us for dinner in the restaurant at six o'clock."

"Okay," I said. "See you for dinner."

Grandma hugged us both. When she left, Julian and I went to our separate rooms to unpack. I neatly folded my clothes and placed them in the drawer. Next, I put my novels and notebook on the desk. I sat by the window and studied the view again. It took my breath away. The hillside, vast and green, flourished with forests and lakes.

"I could live here," I murmured to myself.

When I had finished unpacking, I went to Julian's room. He was putting his clothes away.

"Can I come in?" I asked, standing in the doorway.

"Yes."

I walked in and sat at the foot of the bed. "What do you think?"

"Well, for some reason I was expecting something more… quaint. I had no idea this place would be so luxurious."

"It surprised me too."

"I hope I manage to get some drawing done."

"You'll be inspired in no time."

Julian laughed. "If only…"

"I'm going to go out and explore a bit. Do you want to come?"

He nodded. "Let's go."

We went outside to thoroughly acquaint ourselves with the park-like surroundings. Beneath our shoes, the lush green grass was springy and moist with dew. Towering evergreens shaded our path through the grounds, and a pond lightly rippled in golden, late-afternoon sunlight. The scene before us looked like an impressionist painting.

We walked slowly, taking every exquisite detail in, but not talking much. I didn't feel the need to. It wasn't awkward at all.

When the wind picked up, I shivered, envying the thick jacket Julian wore. "I'm cold," I complained.

"Yeah, it's chilly. The sun is starting to go down already."

"Can I wear your jacket?" I dared ask.

"I'm cold too, you know."

"Pretty please?" I gave him my puppy-dog eyed stare.

"Don't give me that look."

"Why not?"

"Because…" Julian sighed. He shrugged off his jacket and handed it to me. "Here."

Our hands brushed.

I put the jacket on. "So warm," I gushed.

Julian sighed again.

In the lodge's restaurant, a colourful array of small dishes was laid before us. "Wow, that looks so good!" I said, my mouth watering.

"Looks delicious," Julian agreed.

"Our chef, Angie, is incredibly talented. We're so lucky to have her. All our guests are well-fed," Grandma said.

"Help yourselves," Grandpa said, readying his knife and fork.

We filled our plates, and I dug in greedily. We chatted as we ate.

"How's school my dear? Assignments going well?" Grandma asked.

"Yes. I only have a couple left to complete. Then, the rest of the year will be revision for exams."

"You're a hard worker," Grandpa said. "I'm sure you'll pass everything with flying colours."

"I hope so."

"Hill Law will be lucky to have you."

I coughed, choking a little on my food. Julian eyed me expectantly while biting his lip. "Actually, I'm not going to study law anymore," I explained when I had recovered.

"What happened? Did you change your mind?"

I nodded. "I've decided to do the thing I want to do."

"And what's that?"

"I want to write. I'm going to do a creative writing programme." I braced myself for their response.

"That sounds simply wonderful," Grandma said.

I immediately relaxed. "Really? I'm glad you think so. My parents aren't exactly thrilled. They think it's a waste of time."

"Well, I think it's fabulous. Life's too short not to follow your dreams."

Grandpa nodded along. "We know that too well."

"You do?" I asked.

"Do you know what we did before we ran the lodge?"

"No. I don't remember."

"We had corporate jobs. Mary was an admin at a large firm, and I was an accountant. We didn't enjoy our jobs, but we kept our heads down until we eventually retired."

"And then you bought the lodge?"

"Yes. We bought this property and turned it into a bed-and-breakfast. It had always been Mary's dream."

"Our lives changed dramatically since we started running the lodge," Grandma explained. "We're happier than we've ever been. My only regret is we didn't do it sooner. To think of all those wasted years… If you want to be a writer, then I say go for it. Don't leave your dreams until you're old."

Their words encouraged me. "Thanks. I'll do the best I can."

"You know, it's a funny coincidence you want to be a writer," Grandpa said.

"Why?"

"After dinner, I want to show you something."

Julian returned to his room, and I followed Grandpa to the private wing.

"Where are we going?" I asked, curiosity welling inside me.

"To my study," he said as we turned up a staircase.

At the top, he opened a door into a dark room. He flicked on the light switch. The large room was furnished with bookcases and oil paintings. Two worn, brown leather chairs with tufted backs sat atop a faded rug. The room smelled of leather and old books.

"I often spend my evenings here." Grandpa turned on a lamp, illuminating the surface of a mahogany writing desk. Loose papers surrounded a clunky typewriter. Words half-filled a page in the typewriter.

"Are you writing something?" I took a closer look.

Grandpa nodded. He roughly gathered the papers into one stack.

"What is it? A novel?"

"No. My memoirs. It's something I've been wanting to do for a long time. This year, I finally started working on it."

"So, you're a writer too?"

"I suppose I am." Grandpa chuckled. "Isn't it wonderful?"

"It's brilliant. Will you let me read it when you're done?"

"Of course. But you'll have to let me read something of yours in return."

I laughed. "Okay, then. It's a deal."

We were interrupted by a soft knock on the door. I turned my head. Grandma stood in the doorway, holding a thermos and two large mugs.

"Coffee, anyone?"

"Ah, thank you," Grandpa said.

She set the mugs down on the coffee table and poured the steaming hot liquid inside.

"Thanks," I said.

She quietly disappeared again.

"My dear wife brings me a coffee every evening to drink while I write," Grandpa explained. He took a mug and sat down on an armchair. "Make yourself comfortable."

I sat down on the chair next to him, sinking into its buttery softness. I pulled a wool throw over my legs and cradled the warm ceramic mug in my hands.

As Grandpa drank, he wore a distant expression on his face as if he were mulling something over. "You know, Ivy," he said after a few more sips. "When you said you wanted to write, I wasn't surprised at all."

"Why?" I asked, eyebrow raised.

"As a little girl, you were always a storyteller."

"I was?"

Grandpa nodded. "You used to read to me from the books you made. Do you remember? You would write these little stories and poems in handmade booklets. You even did your own illustrations. They were quite good for someone so young."

"I don't remember."

"You had a creative spark in you. That's for sure. Your parents probably didn't nurture it, which is a shame. I'm glad the spark has returned."

"Me too." I couldn't help sighing. "I just wish my parents felt that way."

Grandpa ran a hand through his silver hair. "It's an unfortunate situation to be in. I wish I could do something to help."

"It's okay."

"It's not okay. Ivy, I want you to know you have my full support. No matter what."

A warm tear escaped and slid down my cheek. I brushed it away before he could notice. "Thank you, Grandpa." I walked to him and offered a hug.

He enveloped me in his arms and patted me on the back. "Whatever you decide to pursue, your grandmother and I will be there for you."

"That means a lot to me." More tears escaped, falling to his shoulder and seeping through the fabric.

"There, there."

I breathed in deeply and pulled myself together before sitting back down and finishing my coffee.

"Have you got any plans for tomorrow?" Grandpa asked.

"I was thinking of maybe going for a hike if the weather is okay."

"That sounds like a good idea."

"I'm hoping the view from the mountain will inspire Julian to draw again. He's suffering artist's block."

"Oh, I see. Good thinking."

Despite the caffeine, tiredness caught up with me and I failed to stifle a yawn.

Grandpa chuckled. "It's been a long day. Why don't you go to your room and get some rest?"

I nodded drowsily.

"Goodnight, Ivy."

"Goodnight, Grandpa."

I left Grandpa in the softly lit room and descended the stairs. The lodge halls were quiet and still. When I arrived outside my room, I noticed the light on in Julian's room.

I wonder what he's up to? I reached out to knock but stopped myself. He might be working, and I didn't wish to disturb him.

19

I slipped on my best walking shoes and tied the shoelaces.

Julian waited outside his room. "Are you ready?" he asked.

"Yes. I think so."

Apart from the frost earlier in the morning and some lingering mist, it was a fine day for a hike.

"Be careful out there," Grandma warned before we set out. "There aren't really any proper tracks out that way. You'll need to follow your nose. Cell phone coverage is practically non-existent as well."

"Don't worry. We'll be careful." Truth be told, I wasn't great with directions. I trusted Julian would know what he was doing, though. He seemed confident about the hike.

"Take these," Grandma handed us each a lunchbox filled with goodies from the lodge kitchen.

"Thanks!"

We packed them in our backpacks.

"Have a nice time!"

"I'm sure we will. See you later."

I checked through the gear I had packed once again.

"Are you all set?" Julian asked.

"I think so."

"Let's go, then."

We stepped out into the brisk air. The mountain loomed in the distance, shrouded in mist. It would be a long trek across the grounds just to get near it. I took a deep breath of fresh, moist air, and then strode onward with Julian at my side. We walked a shaded path under the evergreens, silent apart from the rustle of the breeze through the leaves and the tweeting of native birds. The ground was mostly flat, and we made fast progress.

At the edge of the lodge grounds, a wire fence cut off our path. I couldn't see a gate anywhere.

"Can you climb over it?" Julian asked.

"I think so." I reached my leg over, but I wobbled.

Julian steadied me, his hands around my waist. With his help, I managed to clamber over. He followed.

Standing at the base of the mountain, I looked up towards the peak and gulped.

"Having second thoughts?" Julian asked.

I took a deep breath in and shook my head. "Let's do this."

"That's the spirit."

I spotted a faint trail in the grass. "Here. This must be the way."

We tentatively began our ascent. Julian let me set the pace, staying ever so slightly behind.

I tried to make conversation as we walked. "So…are you enjoying your stay so far?" I asked.

"Yup. It's so nice here. You know, I wasn't sure if it was a good idea at first. When I was thinking of taking a break, I pictured something more solitary. But I think this turned out to be just what I needed."

"That's good. I was worried it might be weird for you, spending a holiday with me and my grandparents."

Julian shrugged. "I don't mind at all. Your grandparents seem cool."

"Yeah, they are." The conversation with Grandpa immediately surfaced in my mind, and I smiled.

"It's actually good for me to take a trip with someone. Usually, I spend most of my time alone. I guess I'm a bit of a loner normally."

"Me too."

"You seem close with Lana."

"Uh huh. We've known each other since primary school."

"It's nice to have someone like that. All my friends are off at university. I've fallen out of contact with most of them."

"That sucks."

Julian shrugged. "It can't be helped. Our lives just went in different directions. It's funny to think they'll be graduating this year and going off to work in their high-flying careers." Envy tinged his voice.

"You'll be going overseas to study with a famous Italian artist," I reminded him.

"It could be years before I'm in a stable situation where I can earn a living."

"But at least you'll be doing what you love. Your friends will envy you when they're stuck behind a desk all day in an office and you're off in Europe, visiting galleries and studying classical drawing."

"I guess." He didn't sound convinced.

"Having second thoughts?"

"Constantly. Every day I doubt my talent as an artist."

"Isn't that normal for every artist?"

"Yes." Julian chuckled. "I'm sure you're right. Sorry to vent."

"I don't mind." It was actually comforting to know someone like Julian also had his doubts. He normally seemed so steadfast.

We slowed down for a minute, taking in our surroundings—the ancient trees and overgrown foliage teeming with wildlife. I stared down in awe over the edge of the mountain at the deep green valley filled with swirling mist.

"Sometimes, being out in nature really puts things in perspective, doesn't it? Makes all my worries seem so insignificant," Julian said.

The valley below seemed infinite. I recoiled, feeling dizzy.

"You don't have a fear of heights, do you?" Julian asked, grinning.

"No. I don't think so."

He gave me a gentle shove towards the edge. I yelped and desperately grasped at his jacket.

"You're so mean!"

Before I could retaliate, he broke away and continued onward.

"Wait for me!" I ran to catch up, the overgrown grass brushing against my ankles.

I caught up with him just as we came to a place where gnarled tree roots blocked our path. We scrambled over them.

"How are you doing?" Julian asked.

My legs were beginning to ache. It had been a long time since I'd properly exercised like this. I was really out of practice. Julian seemed to be fine, so I didn't give away that I was already tired.

"I'm okay." I gathered myself and pushed onward despite the stitch in my stomach.

When we emerged through a patch of mist, the summit was suddenly in sight. "We're almost there," I said excitedly. With a newfound burst of energy, I sped up my pace. At the peak, I stopped to catch my breath.

A spectacular view looking over the nearby towns, lakes and rivers spread out in front of us. "You can see so much from up here!"

Julian stood by my side. "It's beautiful." He sighed.

When I had recovered from my sense of awe, I spread out a blanket on the grass and sat down. It was a huge relief to my sore legs and feet. Julian joined me, and we unpacked our lunchboxes. Each lunchbox contained an apple, crackers and cheese, a sandwich made with homemade bread, and a cookie. I was ravenous, wolfing down the sandwich within a few bites and then the cookie. I saved the rest for later.

"Shall we head back?" Julian asked, after we had finished lunch.

I shook my head. "Let's stay for a while. If you don't mind." I needed longer to recover before the downward journey.

"That's fine. Actually, this is a good opportunity to try to get some sketching done. I don't get to see scenery like this very often."

"Good idea."

He took a large sketchbook and a pencil case from his bag. He opened the sketchbook on his lap, selected a pencil, and got to work.

While Julian sketched, I lay on the blanket, reading a book. Every now and then, I looked up from my novel to watch his progress. His drawing was very rough, but with every stroke of graphite, a stronger image emerged. When he had finished, he flicked to a new page, moved to a different position, and started the process again.

I finished my book, so I lay back and relaxed, watching the clouds slowly drift across the sky. They lulled me. My thoughts grew hazy, and my eyelids fluttered shut.

Disoriented, I scanned the hilltop searching for Julian. He stood upon the edge of a cliff.

"Julian?" I asked.

He turned to me, smiling. "Let's go," he said, voice gentle.

I walked over. "Where are we going?"

"There's no time to explain." He took my hand. "Are you ready?"

"I think so."

"Good." Pulling me with him, he stepped over the edge.

I closed my eyes tight, expecting to fall, but we floated.

"See?" Julian said. We drifted weightlessly above the treetops.

"This is wonderful!"

"Here." Julian led us to a clearing in the trees. Our feet touched down on the soft grass. "You're safe now." He enveloped me in his arms.

Suddenly, everything began to shake. I jolted awake with a start. Julian lay beside me on the blanket. His jacket was draped over us.

"How long was I asleep?" I asked.

"Just a few minutes. I was worried you would get cold, though."

"Sorry." I returned his jacket.

"What were you dreaming about? You looked peaceful."

"It was a nice dream," I admitted.

"Oh yeah? Was I in it?" Julian joked.

I blushed, lost for words. After such a long pause, I couldn't deny the obvious truth.

Julian studied me, biting his lip as his warm breath brushed against my cheek. "You'll have to tell me about it sometime," he almost whispered.

I gazed into his deep green eyes, searching for a hint of what he was feeling. Just when I thought it would be safe to move closer, Julian broke away.

"The sun is starting to set," he said.

I looked up at the sky marbled with streaks of pink. "It must be getting late," I said, getting to my feet. "We better head back, or it will get dark before we reach the lodge."

Julian agreed.

We gathered our things and were about to head off, but I became disorientated. I had completely lost any sense of direction.

"Uh, Julian, do you know which way we came from?"

Julian looked just as clueless as I felt.

"I think…it's this way." Julian gestured left. "But I'm not sure."

"Neither am I," I said.

We scrutinised our surroundings, looking for clues as the sunlight rapidly declined.

"Let's just go," I said. "I trust you."

"You shouldn't trust me, but what choice do we have? We're both not sure."

We started our descent. Parts of the journey brought back memories, and I felt like we were heading in the right direction. But then the scenery became unfamiliar.

"I don't think this is the right way," I said.

"It's too late to turn back now. We need to reach the bottom before it gets dark."

I felt like we should be worried, but with Julian by my side, I somehow felt safe.

The descent was much more painless than the climb. When we reached the bottom, we found ourselves on an unknown road.

"Where to from here?" I asked.

"Let's walk down the road until we find a landmark. Then we might get a sense of where we are."

"Good plan."

The road was quiet. Cars only passed by every now and then. Eventually, we arrived at a very small township.

"Do you know where we are?" Julian asked. "Does this look familiar to you?"

I shook my head. "I haven't been here before. It can't be too far away, though. Maybe I can call my grandparents and get them to pick us up?"

"Yeah. We better try to contact them."

I took my phone out of my backpack. The screen was blank and holding the power button did nothing. "Crap. It's completely dead. I don't remember their phone number by heart either."

"Well, let's ask someone around here if they know the way to the lodge?"

I nodded.

A corner store stood across the road. "Let's ask in there."

We crossed the road and entered the small shop. It sold magazines, chocolate bars and ice creams. That was pretty much the extent of it. At first, I couldn't see a shopkeeper anywhere, but then he emerged from the back room.

"Excuse me?" I asked.

"Yes?"

"Do you know the way to Landsend Lodge?"

The shopkeeper nodded. "You need directions?"

"Yeah. We're just a bit lost."

"Do you have a car?"

"No. We're on foot."

"Oh?" The shopkeeper realigned a wonky chocolate bar. "You can get there by foot, but it's difficult to explain. I'll write it down."

"Thank you. That would be great."

The shopkeeper took a pen and a notepad from behind the counter. He scribbled down the directions. "I hope you can read my writing."

He tore off the piece of paper and handed it to me. The writing looked legible enough and was accompanied by a crude diagram.

"Thanks again," I said.

We left the shop. After a quick stop at the public restroom, we continued our journey back to the lodge. Directions in hand, we finally found ourselves back in familiar territory. The day had turned pitch black now, and it was freezing cold. My teeth chattered.

"Do you want to wear my jacket?" Julian asked.

"No, that's fine. It's cold. You need it."

Julian took it off anyway and wrapped it over my shoulders. "You need it more than me."

We arrived at the Landsend Lodge sign and began the trek up the long, steep, gravel driveway. "Almost there," I said with relief when the lodge finally came into view. I quickened my pace, desperate to get back. In my haste, I made a misstep and my ankle rolled. I shrieked with pain.

Julian stopped in his tracks. "Are you okay?"

"I'm fine," I croaked unconvincingly. I gathered myself and limped a few steps forward.

"You don't look fine."

"I'm okay."

"Ivy—"

"Huh?"

Julian bent down with his back towards me. "Hop on."

"What?" I spluttered.

"Get on my back."

I hesitated. *A piggy back with Julian?* My cheeks blazed at the thought.

"Come on."

I tentatively took a step towards him.

"Lean against me. Put your arms around my shoulders."

I did as he said, pressing my weight to his back. In one swift movement, he scooped me up off the ground, seemingly with ease. He walked forward. I held on tight.

"Would you relax? I'm not going to let you fall."

"Sorry." I tried to loosen my vice-like grip.

Soon enough, I was at ease, safe and secure in his arms. I let my head rest on his shoulder and closed my eyes. Julian didn't say anything. He walked on without complaint. Even when we reached the lodge, he continued to carry me all the way to my room.

He gently let me down outside the door. "Are you okay?" he asked again.

"I think so. It's just a twisted ankle."

"Try not to put too much weight on it."

I nodded. "Thank you for the piggy back."

"It's fine. I couldn't let you walk in that condition."

We lingered awkwardly at my door. Julian chewed his lip, and I wondered what he was thinking about.

"Well…" I began.

Julian lifted his head. "Hmmm?"

"I think I'll go and have a lie down."

"That's a good idea. I'm pretty tired too."

"I don't know if I'll see you again tonight."

"That's okay. Get some rest."

I nodded.

Julian retreated, leaving me alone. In my room, I collapsed in a heap on the bed, exhausted from the day.

20

I awoke the next morning to bright sunlight streaming in through the crack between the curtains. I got up and stretched. My muscles still ached from all the walking the previous day. After getting dressed, I went to the restaurant for breakfast. A few other guests dined, mostly older couples. I didn't see Julian and assumed he must have already eaten. I had blueberry pancakes and a strong cup of coffee.

After breakfast, I went outside to enjoy the sun. Julian sat on a deck chair, a sketchbook in his lap. Thrilled he was drawing again, I decided not to disturb him. Instead, I enjoyed a stroll around the gardens. As I took in the beauty of the fragrant winter blooms, I felt a deep sense of calm.

Venturing deeper into a wooded area, I came across an old shed nestled among the trees. A rusted padlock hung on the door, but it wasn't locked. With a couple of heaves, it swung open. The shed housed a solitary table and chair. Cobwebs glistened in every corner. Sun streamed in the window, revealing dust in the air and casting stripes of light on the floorboards. The room smelled of cedar wood and moss.

I sat down at the small table. This would make a good place to write, completely private and utterly peaceful. I leaned my head on the table and felt myself grow drowsy. A blackbird flew inside, beating its wings in a flurry, startling me. I shooed the bird outside and closed the door.

As I made my way back to the building, I saw Grandpa out watering the garden. "Morning, Grandpa."

"Morning, Ivy. How are you enjoying your stay?"

"I'm loving it. It's so beautiful here."

"That's good. I'm glad you're having a nice time."

"Do you need any help with the gardening?"

"So kind of you to offer. Actually, I'm not so good with bending down at my age. If you could pull out those weeds, that would be very helpful indeed."

I rolled up my jeans and got down on my knees. The soil was soft and moist beneath me. I began to pull out the weeds.

"There's an awful lot of work involved in keeping the grounds maintained, we have a landscaper who comes in once a month, but between that, your grandmother and I do most of the upkeep."

"That must be hard on you."

"It sure is. To be honest, we're starting to get a bit too old for it. We've been thinking of hiring someone as a live-in groundskeeper to take some of the pressure off us. They could mow the lawns, water the garden and sweep the paths. That kind of thing."

"That sounds like a good idea to me. You can't keep doing all this work forever."

"It's certainly kept us young, but I think it's getting to the point where this would be a good option."

"I think so too."

When I had finished pulling the weeds, we moved on to

the next section of the garden. "I had a nice walk around the grounds just before. I saw the old shed in that patch of trees over there."

"You did?" Grandpa chuckled. "I have a soft spot for that shed. Your grandma wanted to demolish it, but I think it has a lot of character. I would like to convert it into a private cabin for guests one day."

"That's a good idea. It's in a beautiful spot."

"I used to retreat there, every now and then, for a bit of privacy. But I haven't done so in quite some time."

"If you ever convert it, let me know. I would love to see it."

"I'll bring it up again with your grandma. Perhaps this is the year."

After helping Grandpa with the gardening, I walked over to Julian. He was still sitting in the same spot, pen and sketchbook in hand.

"Hi." I pulled up a chair beside him.

"Hey."

I saw the picture he was drawing. A gorgeous rendering of the large, weeping willow tree and the duck pond. "That's amazing."

"Thanks. Yeah, I'm feeling pretty good about it. I don't usually draw landscapes, but I'm getting better at it."

"So, you're no longer blocked?"

"Yeah. I think I'm through it. Thanks to this trip."

"That's good! Now, you'll be able to finish your portfolio."

Julian nodded. He put his sketchbook down. "How are you holding up after yesterday?"

"My ankle seems fine now. I'm still pretty sore all over, though."

"Yeah? Me too."

"It didn't help that we got lost."

"No, it didn't." He laughed.

"Hot drink anyone?" Grandma appeared behind us with a thermos.

"Yes, please," Julian and I said in unison.

The hot coffee warmed me up. Despite the sunshine, a wintery chill lingered in the air. When I began to get too cold, I went inside to enjoy the warmth and comfort of the library. I sank into an armchair and read for several hours.

I was deeply absorbed in reading until Grandma entered the room.

"There you are," she said. "I was looking for you."

"Sorry."

"I was going to do some baking, and I thought you'd like to help. You used to love it when you were a child."

"I'd love to help." I put the book away and followed Grandma to her private kitchen. Large cupboards and benches equipped the farmhouse style kitchen. Copper pots and pans hung above an island counter in the centre.

"I bake every day. I like to leave treats for the guests," Grandma explained.

"What are we going to bake?"

"Your favourite."

"Chocolate chip cookies?"

Grandma nodded.

I was as excited as a little kid. Mum never baked, so this was a rare opportunity.

Grandma read out a list of ingredients, and I sourced them from the huge walk-in pantry.

"How have you enjoyed your stay?" Grandma asked while she mixed the ingredients together.

"It's been so relaxing. I don't want to leave."

"And what about Julian?"

"He's had a good time too. I think the trip has helped him get over his artists' block."

"That's good. He's a talented young man. So handsome too." Grandma eyed me knowingly. "He must like you a lot to come here with you. Is he your boyfriend?"

"No. We're just friends," I explained again.

"But you'd like to be more than friends?"

"Grandma! This is way too embarrassing."

"I can tell by the way you look at him."

"You can?"

Grandma nodded. "I was around your age when I started seeing Arnold."

"You married quite young, didn't you?"

"I was twenty."

"Only two years older than me..."

Grandma formed the cookie dough into balls, pressing them onto a greased tray. I helped her, scooping some dough from the bowl.

"I think you and Julian would make a cute couple," Grandma said wistfully. "Let me know if anything happens between you two."

"Nothing's going to happen."

"Whatever you say," Grandma said teasingly.

I ate so many cookies, I almost didn't have any room for dinner. Fortunately, when the roast meal was laid out before us, I grew hungry again. Grandpa filled our glasses with red wine.

"I want to thank you for letting us stay. I've had a really nice time," I said.

Julian murmured in agreement.

"Not a problem at all, my dear," Grandma said. "In fact, we'd love it if you came more often. Isn't that right, Arnold?"

"Indeed," Grandpa said. "It has been a pleasure having you."

Grandma filled my plate and I began to eat, savouring every bite.

After dinner, Julian and I headed back to our rooms.

"Ivy?" Julian said when we reached our doors.

"Yes?"

"It's still early."

"Yeah."

"Do you want to come in?" he asked, motioning to his door.

"Huh?"

A blush crept onto his cheeks. "I mean, I've been on a roll with my art lately, and I'd like to draw you."

"Okay, sure."

"Then let's go inside." Julian directed me into his room and closed the door behind us.

"It's been a while since I modelled for you."

"Yeah."

"Where do you want me?"

Julian opened the sliding door out onto the balcony. The brisk air swept in. "Stand out here. I know it's cold, but this will be a quick sketch."

"Okay." I stood outside.

True to his word, Julian whipped out a pen and his sketchbook, and very quickly and loosely, he sketched me.

"Can I look?" I asked when he had finished.

Julian showed me the sketch. It was far from perfect, but it had a liveliness to it I had not seen in his work before.

"It's good. I think you've nailed it."

"Can I draw one more picture?"

"Yes."

I sat at the foot of the bed. He brought his pen down to the page but stopped abruptly. He approached me.

"Your hair's in your face."

His hand came down and he gently tucked a strand behind my ear. The feeling of his hand on my skin made me weak. His hand lingered, and I looked into his eyes, wondering what he was thinking. He looked back at me, and I thought I saw longing in his eyes. My heart beat fast in my chest. My eyes wandered to his lips. I began to tilt my head.

This is actually happening.

A ring tone began to sound. Julian's phone vibrated on the coffee table. The screen read *Charlotte Preston*. I prayed Julian wouldn't answer it, but he snapped away from me and picked up the phone.

"I have to take this." He left me alone in his room, taking the call in the hallway.

I withered in my seat. Something good was about to happen, then one call ruined it all. Charlotte Preston was more important. For some reason, I had thought she was out of the picture.

I couldn't hear what Julian was saying. When he re-emerged, he looked solemn.

"What was that about?"

Julian hesitated. "It's nothing."

I didn't press further.

Julian paced back and forth a few times.

"Are you going to finish the drawing?" I asked.

Julian shook his head. "Maybe we should call it a night."

My grandparents took us to the airport the next morning. When we said our goodbyes, I almost cried.

Grandpa wiped away an errant tear with his handkerchief. "You'll be missed," he said.

"Come back soon!" Grandma said.

"I will."

I kept turning back to wave to them as we waited in the queue to board.

Few words were exchanged between Julian and I during the flight. Upon our arrival, he offered me a stiff, awkward hug before we went our separate ways. It stung. I tried to hide my hurt. Why was he acting so cold?

When I arrived home, I went to my room. The wall calendar plastered above my desk reminded me of the important dates which loomed. Mock exams and the due date of my application to Elias. There wasn't much time left.

21

As soon as I stepped through the school gate, Lana was drawn to me like a magnet, inundating me with questions about my time at the lodge with Julian.

"I want all the details," she stressed.

After I gave her a brief rundown, Lana seemed confused. "Does that mean Julian and Charlotte are a couple?"

"I don't know. If they are, he's a jerk. I mean, he almost kissed me."

"There must be some other explanation…"

Before we could ruminate any further, the bell rang.

Part way through my economics lesson, I was summoned to see the careers adviser, who I learnt was called Ms. Edmond. I left class and made my way to the careers office.

"Miss Beckett?" Ms. Edmond looked up from the file in front of her. It had my name on it.

"Yes." I approached her, feeling a little nervous.

"Take a seat."

I put my bag on the floor and sat down.

"As you know, all students have an appointment with me in their final year to discuss their future career path."

I nodded. "I visited a while ago to get some info on the Elias Institute."

Ms. Edmond adjusted her glasses and peered at me. "That's right. Creative writing was it?"

"Yes. I've decided to apply."

"It's a good school. As I'm sure you're aware, arts degrees aren't very marketable today, but most Elias students don't struggle to find employment. Have you thought about possible career outcomes?"

"Outcomes?"

"What do you want to do once you graduate Elias?"

I had a complete mind blank. Heat blossomed to my cheeks.

Ms. Edmond prompted me again. "Is there a particular career or job you would like to do?"

"I don't know," I finally admitted. "I haven't thought too much about it."

"Then I recommend you give this more thought, Miss Beckett. It may seem like the far-off future, but it will come around much faster than you think."

"Okay. I'll think about it."

"The good news is you will have three more years to figure it out. I'm sure Elias will offer plenty of career support."

"I'll try take advantage of it."

"Good. I recommend you do so." Ms. Edmond made a note in my file. "Have you applied for a student loan?"

"Not yet, but I plan to."

"Were you aware Elias requires a one-thousand-dollar deposit upon acceptance? It will be reimbursed once the student loan kicks in, but initially, you will have to pay for it from your own pocket."

"No. I didn't know that."

"Will that be a problem?"

"It might be. I don't think my parents will pay for it, and I don't have enough money to pay for it by myself."

"Do you have any other family members who might offer you a loan?"

I thought of my kind old grandparents. "Possibly."

"There is also the issue of living costs. Wellington has a fairly high cost of living. Are you eligible for a student allowance?"

"I don't know."

"How much do your parents earn?"

"No idea. They don't tell me things like that."

"Are your parents full-time professionals?"

"Yes."

"Then it's highly unlikely you qualify."

"Oh."

"You can always claim living costs on your loan, but the amount is unlikely to cover all your expenses. Can your parents support you at all?"

"No. They're not going to support me."

"Elias students are discouraged from having part-time jobs due to the intensive nature of the course. In your case, it might be the only way you'll be able to cover your costs."

"Yes, I thought that would be the case."

"Do you have any work experience?"

"I did some work experience at a law firm, but apart from that, I've never had a job."

Ms. Edmond took down more notes. "You might find it

difficult to find part-time employment without retail or hospitality experience."

"Would it help if I found a summer job?"

"Yes, I think it would."

"What about scholarships? Are there any I might be eligible for?"

"Elias offers one full scholarship per course every year. You're obviously a bright girl, but these scholarships are highly competitive. Only the most exceptional students stand a chance."

That counts me out, then.

"You'll also need to consider the cost of accommodation. Elias does not offer their own student accommodation, but there are plenty of options nearby." Ms. Edmond pulled out several brochures for apartment buildings and handed them to me.

I had a quick flick through. Seeing the costs gave me a fright. Most of them cost more per week than I would be able to get from a student loan. I gulped.

"Is there anything cheaper than this?"

"There is cheaper accommodation outside the city centre, but then you need to factor in transport costs as well."

I felt so disheartened I was on the brink of tears.

Ms. Edmond reached out a hand and patted me on the shoulder in a feeble attempt to comfort me. "Ivy, I admire that you want to follow your heart and study something you love, but it seems like you haven't fully thought this through."

"It was a recent decision to apply. I haven't thought over the finer details yet."

"If you want my advice, I would not rush into this. I would take a year or two, get a job, save up and then apply."

Her sensible advice fell heavy on my ears.

"Otherwise, if you can study something your parents will support, that would also be a good option. You will probably have better career outcomes as well."

I nodded along.

I left the meeting feeling fragile. Ms. Edmond's words had made me feel dumb.

I confided in Lana at lunch time.

"Don't listen to that old bat," she said. "What does she know about university and careers? She has been working as a part-time careers adviser at a high school since before we were born. What real-world experience does she have?"

Lana raised a valid point, but I still felt uncertain. "What if she's right?"

"You can find a way to make it work."

"I hope so."

"Thousands of students have pulled it off before. Why can't you?"

"Thanks, Lana. I really needed a pep talk."

She slapped me on the back. "No problem. Now, get that application in before it's too late."

By midnight, I had typed the final sentence of the short story I was to submit with my application to Elias. Too tired to go back and read through it, I hit print.

I took the document to Mr. Donaldson after class the next day.

"What's this?" he asked.

"It's the writing sample I'm going to submit with my Elias application. I was hoping you could critique it."

"Ah, good. I was wondering when you would take up my

offer." He took the document and flicked through it. "What's it about?"

"It's a mystery, with a hint of surrealism. Actually, I was inspired a lot by *Hole Hearted*."

Mr. Donaldson laughed. "I'm glad to have had such an influence on you. I will read it at once and prepare some notes."

The next day, Mr. Donaldson wordlessly slipped a manila folder on my desk. My stomach twisted in knots.

22

I couldn't bring myself to review Mr. Donaldson's notes until after school. I fished for the manila folder in my bag. With a deep breath, I opened it and a memo fell out.

Ivy,

Thank you for entrusting me with this task. I read your piece with fervour. Please see my comments within.

AD

Nerves swimming in my stomach, I opened the document. The swathe of red ink hit me straight in the gut. I felt like my worst fears had been confirmed.

It's shit. I'm a terrible writer. I'll never get into Elias.

Pull yourself together, I told myself.

It took all the courage I could muster, but I read through each excruciating comment. My brain became overwhelmed, and I couldn't process anything. I had to put it aside.

After dinner, I reluctantly picked it back up again.

I have to do this. Strong coffee in hand and my laptop open on the dining room table, I began to tackle the extensive revisions which lay ahead.

Several hours and coffees later, I finally began to see improvement in my story. I just needed to give it one more push.

"Ivy?" Dad asked from the doorway. "What are you doing up so late?"

"I need to finish editing my story. My application is due soon."

Dad poured himself a glass of water. "You should be in bed. Teenagers need all the sleep they can get."

"I'm fine," I said, yawning.

"Well, it's nice to see you working so hard at something."

"I'm nearly done."

Dad sighed. "It's okay. I know this is important to you. Stay up as late as you need to. I won't tell your mother."

"Thanks, Dad. Goodnight."

"Night night, sweetheart." Dad left me in peace.

As much as I tried to resist it, I began to succumb to tiredness. I did as much as I could before going to bed.

When I returned to the story the next day, I read it through once, and that was enough.

It's done.

I clasped an A4 envelope, my application to Elias enclosed. I was about to leave to post it, but Mum held me back.

"Please, just consider it," she said, a pleading look in her eyes. "What if you don't get in? What if you need a back-up plan?" Mum thrust another envelope at me. "Just take it. It wouldn't hurt."

I cautiously took the envelope and inspected it. It wasn't sealed, so I removed the contents and rifled through it.

"I took the liberty of finishing it off for you."

"What?"

"Our handwriting is similar. You can't tell."

It was true. It had been so long since I had touched the Law School application, and looking through it now, I couldn't tell what I had written and what was Mum's effort. I put it back in the envelope.

"Fine. I'll take it." I grabbed the cellotape and taped it shut.

Mum exhaled with relief.

"It won't make any difference anyway," I added on my way out of the door. I didn't give her a chance to respond.

At the post office box, I slipped my Elias application through the slot. I hesitated on the Law School application. I wished I hadn't given in to Mum. Now, I had given her false hope.

Never mind. I shoved the envelope through the slot with unnecessary force. At least this would get her off my case for a while. For that alone, it was worth it. Walking back home empty-handed, I felt an immense sense of relief. I had done it. I had really applied to my dream school. I couldn't wait to tell Lana the news.

And Julian, I thought, though the prospect of contacting him made me feel ill. I still had no idea where we stood.

I tried calling Lana first, but there was no answer. I texted her the good news instead.

Hey, Lana. Sent my application to Elias today :) I feel like celebrating! Let me know if you're free tonight.

I wrote a text to Julian as well, but promptly deleted it. I didn't feel like making the first move. *It is up to him,* I stubbornly decided.

I waited the rest of the day for Lana to reply. I tried calling her too. No luck. I thought that was weird. Perhaps she had a big shift at the hospital. Oh well, I would see her at school the next day.

Except, I didn't.

Lana did not turn up at school. I asked Miss April if she knew why Lana was absent.

"She's sick," she replied. "If you ask me, she's overworked. Hopefully, she recovers in time for the mock exams."

I continued to try to contact Lana with no success. When she did not turn up at school the next day, or the next after that, I went to her house.

Mrs. Wu let me in after a lengthy period of deliberation. "She's in her room. If she's asleep, don't rouse her," she warned.

Jack and Bing ran past me in the hallway, laughing between themselves. Mrs. Wu scolded them as I climbed the stairs. I carefully opened the door to Lana's room. She lay in bed, awake but still.

"Lana," I said, my voice just above a whisper.

She turned over. Her face lit up the moment her eyes fell on me. "Ivy! I would get up and hug you if only I had the energy."

"Are you okay? What happened?"

"I thought I got struck down with a bug, but the doctor said it's exhaustion. The cure? I have to rest up. I'm not allowed to do anything except sleep, eat and read. Mum even confiscated my phone and computer. She doesn't want me getting overstimulated."

"That explains why you weren't answering my texts..."

"I'm sorry about that."

"That's okay. I was just worried about you."

"I'll be okay. I'm taking the rest of the week off, but I'm sure I'll be allowed to go back to school next week."

"What about the hospital?"

"I was told to stop working there for now."

"So, will you?"

Lana shrugged. "I'll see how I feel."

"Oh, Lana." I bent down and gave her a hug. She felt clammy in my arms.

"I feel dreadful," she murmured. "Cheer me up. Tell me everything's okay between you and Julian?"

I sat on the edge of her bed, my back to her. "We haven't been in touch since we got back."

"Have you texted him?"

I shook my head.

"Well, what are you waiting for?"

"I don't know. I guess I just feel like waiting for him to make the first move."

"What if he's waiting for *you* to make the first move?"

"I doubt it."

"It wouldn't hurt to try."

I heaved a sigh and slumped down next to her. "I suppose you're right."

"Where's your phone?"

"In my pocket."

"Take it out."

"What?"

"You're going to do this."

"Right now?"

"Yes."

I sighed and took out my phone. "What do I say?"

"Hi, Julian. Haven't heard from you for a while. Do you want to catch up some time?"

I typed the message into my phone, my heart pounding. My finger hovered above the button to send. Before second thoughts could set in, I closed my eyes and pressed send.

Message sent.

"There. Doesn't that feel better?"

"No. Not really."

"Trust me. This is for the best."

"I trust you."

We waited several minutes to see if he would reply. He didn't. Lana's certainty began to dissipate. I changed the subject.

"So, I sent in my application to Elias."

"You did? That's great. That school will be amazing for you."

"Yeah. I think so too. What about you? Is your med school application in yet?"

Lana shook her head. "The deadline's still a while away."

"But everything's under control?"

"Yes. All my scholarship applications are in too. I've already been notified of making the shortlist for one of them."

"Really? That's awesome."

"Thanks," Lana said, blushing slightly.

Mrs. Wu entered the room and cleared her throat. "Ivy, thank you for visiting, but it's now time for Lana to get some more rest."

Lana was about to protest, but I hushed her. "I'll see you soon."

"Let me know what he says."

I nodded once before leaving the room. Mrs. Wu guided me to the front door.

~

Any sense of hope I had evaporated when Julian didn't reply to my text message that day. He was usually quick to respond, so I knew something was wrong. I felt so helpless. I felt a sense of loss—which was funny because I never really had him in the first place. Lana was still sans phone, so I couldn't tell her. *Oh well.* I didn't feel like talking about it just yet anyway.

I went to bed early, exhausted. Sleep washed over me heavy and deep. When I woke up, I momentarily panicked. I had overslept. It took me a moment to realise it was Saturday. I shut Julian out of my mind and decided to pour myself into my studies. Mock exams were a week away. They were important, not just as practice for the real thing. Scholarships and school prizes were often dependent on the results since the final exam results came out too late to count.

I spent the weekend holed up with textbooks and past years' exam papers. It really took my mind off Julian, and I got a lot of work done. By Monday, I was feeling much better. Lana arrived back at school like a whirlwind. It seemed like she had never been ill. She went from class to class with a bounce in her step. She had somehow managed to catch up on everything she missed in one weekend.

We spent much of our time at the library, in the study area on the mezzanine floor. Normally empty throughout the rest of the year, the floor now housed a number of keen students.

"You're working hard," Lana said.

I looked up from my textbook. "Is that surprising?"

"No. Well, yes. A little."

I usually just relied on my natural aptitude for tests rather than partaking in any actual study. "Study has been like a reprieve."

"I see. To stop you thinking about...*him*." Lana cast her glance downwards. "I'm sorry."

"What for?"

"I was so sure he liked you. I really thought..."

"It's okay. I thought so too. For a while. Anyway, let's not talk about that anymore."

We put our heads down and went back to work.

When I got home from school that day, I put my feet up and turned the TV on—a rare occurrence for me. My phone buzzed on the coffee table. I grabbed it, startled when it continued to vibrate in my hand. Someone was calling me.

Julian.

23

"Hello?" I answered, nervously.

"Ivy, it's me." Julian's voice was deep and slightly husky.

"Did you get my text the other day?" I asked.

"Yes, I did. I'm sorry I didn't reply."

"Is everything okay?"

"Yes," he said, although he didn't sound certain. "When would you like to catch up?"

So, it was happening after all.

"This isn't really a good time," I said, coolly. "Mock exams are next week, and I have to study."

"Oh. I see. Well, what about after your exams?"

"That would work."

"Great, well, I'll be in touch. I hope the exams go well."

"Thanks."

"See ya."

"Bye."

Despite the fact Julian had sounded so cold and measured, I still felt excited by the prospect of seeing him again. Perhaps he would finally reveal to me all that was going on.

I called Lana immediately to report the latest news. She was even more ecstatic than I was. "I knew it!" she squealed.

After the call, I tried to concentrate on studying, but my thoughts were on Julian.

On the first day of mock exams, a crowd of Year Thirteen students gathered outside the entrance to the school hall. Everyone chatted nervously. I felt reasonably confident. The only thing making me nervous was the fact Lana had not shown up yet. I checked my watch at 8:54am. The calculus mock exam was to start at 9:00am. I tried not to let Lana's lateness rattle me.

The minutes passed. At 8:59am, Lana had yet to turn up. I looked around, hoping to see her elsewhere in the crowd, but I couldn't find her. I checked my phone. No word from her by 9:00am. The teacher hadn't let us into the hall yet.

At precisely 9:02am, the doors to the hall opened, and the flood of students poured through. I sat at a random desk and watched the rest of the students come through the doors. Lana was not among them. The doors were being closed, but then they lurched to a halt to let one last straggler through.

Lana was white and quivering all over. I wondered if she were feeling sick again. She took her seat. I didn't have much time to wonder. Mr. Sanderson stood on the stage and began his spiel, and a three-hour timer was set. Lana was there, and I was sure she would do a good job. She always did.

I opened my exam booklet and began. All the formulae were firmly entrenched in my brain and the answers came easily. I zoomed through the first paper. Confidence surged in me as I continued on a roll. I sat back, entwined my fingers, pulled my wrists back with a crack and then continued.

A loud, tumbling thud startled everyone. Heads turned, I heard a murmur, then gasps arose. Mr. Sanderson looked up from the lectern, concern washing over his face. He paused the timer.

I looked to the source of the upheaval. Lana lay in a heap on the lino floor, unmoving.

24

I stood up immediately, my pen dropping to the floor and landing with a clack. Mr. Sanderson sped down the aisle to Lana's side. I followed him.

"Everyone, stay back." His outstretched arm stopped me from coming any closer to Lana's limp form. He pressed a thumb to her wrist and checked her pulse.

Each passing second felt like an eternity. *Please,* I prayed. *Let her be okay.*

"Her pulse is normal," he declared at last.

I stopped holding my breath, relief flooding me.

"Lana?" he asked, gently shaking her shoulder. She did not respond. He took out his phone and called emergency services.

A few other teachers arrived, and they collectively agreed to cancel the exam and dismiss everyone. I waited anxiously in the hall with Lana. Some other students stayed behind as well —probably more out of curiosity than concern. An ambulance arrived shortly. Two paramedics entered the hall. They examined Lana and tried to get her to wake.

"Is she going to be okay?" I asked one of the paramedics.

"Her vital signs are normal, but she's still unresponsive. We'll take her to the hospital as a precaution."

"She was sick a couple weeks ago. She was suffering from exhaustion. Do you think that's connected?"

"Yes. That would make a lot of sense. Her energy level is severely low. She is suffering from either not eating enough, not sleeping enough, or both."

Lana did wake, but she wasn't fully lucid. The paramedics put her on a stretcher, ready to take her in the ambulance.

"Can I go with her?" I asked.

"An adult should go with her," Mr. Sanderson explained. "I will go. Maybe someone else can give you a lift?"

Miss April stepped forward. "I'll take you."

"Are you sure?"

Miss April nodded. "Come on. Let's go."

I followed her to the carpark and her beat-up, old Beetle. We puttered along after the ambulance.

After arriving at the hospital, Miss April led the way. "We're looking for Lana Wu," she told the receptionist. "She just arrived by ambulance."

"Certainly. Through the doors on the left, follow the corridor down and straight through the door."

"Thank you."

We pushed through the double doors and walked quickly down the corridor. We came to a large room with hospital beds lining each side, some with green curtains drawn around them. Lana lay, alert but sleepy, in a bed on the left. A doctor was taking tests and asking Mr. Sanderson a lot of questions.

I stood back and let the doctor do her job. I could tell Lana was glad to see me, though. When the doctor left, Mr. Sanderson and Miss April went to get something to eat and drink. I sat on a chair next to Lana.

"How are you doing?" I asked.

Lana looked at me, wide-eyed. "I need to get back and finish the exam."

"No, you don't. The exam has been cancelled."

"But how will I get into Med School?"

I hushed her. The doctor must have given her some kind of drug. "Everything's going to be all right."

Lana began to ease.

Her parents arrived soon after, looking frantic. The doctor returned to explain the situation and calm Mrs. Wu down.

I stayed by Lana's side until the doctor gave her the all clear to go home. She was not to participate in any more mock exams, and not to return to school until after the holidays. No working at the hospital and no extra-curricular activities for the rest of the year. Her parents were to strictly control and monitor her eating and sleeping habits.

Lana took it on the chin, but I was sure she was simply too weak to put up a fight.

Lana's parents dropped me at home.

"Thank you for keeping Lana company," Mrs. Wu said.

"I couldn't leave her," I said. "She's my best friend."

"I know I don't always show it, but I'm glad Lana has you as a friend."

It must have been hard for Mrs. Wu to admit that. I offered a simple nod and a thank you as I left the car.

The day's events had left me utterly exhausted. I really needed someone to talk to, and without giving it much thought, I called Julian. He answered straight away.

"Hey, it's me," I said, my voice breaking.

"Ivy? Are you all right?"

"No. Not really."

"Tell me everything."

25

Julian agreed to meet me at Eastern Park the next day. The park was lined with blossoming trees, and a carpet of pink petals covered the ground. Swans and ducks floated on the pond. I walked to the rotunda in the centre of the park. Julian stood below the white arch. He looked stunning as usual, wearing jeans, a white t-shirt and a brown leather jacket. He leaned casually against the fence.

"Hey," I said, approaching him.

He looked down at me, a smile crossing his lips. I was tempted to go in for a hug, but I cancelled at the last second. It would be too awkward.

"Hey," he said. "It's been a while."

"Yes. We've been busy."

"Do you want a coffee? An ice cream?"

"Oh, yes please. A coffee would be nice."

We went to the kiosk where Julian ordered and paid for two coffees. We sat on the rotunda steps, cradling the hot take-away coffee cups in our hands.

"How's Lana?" Julian asked, his eyebrows creased with

concern.

"I haven't heard from her again since the hospital. I'm sure her parents are looking after her."

"You sounded pretty upset yesterday."

"I got such a fright…"

"It's okay." Julian squeezed my hand. His touch was warm.

"Thanks for seeing me."

"Any time."

"Really?"

Julian nodded. "I know things have been weird lately…"

"It didn't seem like you wanted to speak to me…after the lodge."

Julian's expression turned solemn. "I know. I think I owe you an explanation."

"I just want to know what's up."

He breathed in deeply. "The truth is, I was so caught up in getting my portfolio done."

I could tell that was only part of the reason.

"And Charlotte…" he continued.

Ah, now we're getting to it.

"She didn't want me to tell anyone, but I guess it would be okay to tell you. You don't really know her."

"No, I don't."

"The thing with Charlotte is she seems to have it all together. But, in reality, it's a different story."

"What do you mean?"

"She's in a downward spiral. Depressed, broke, on the brink of dropping out of uni… There's a lot going on in her life. I'm worried about her."

"I had no idea." My feelings were a strange mix of guilt and jealousy.

"I've been trying to support her. We've been friends for a long time. I can't let her down."

"Is she your girlfriend?" I blurted.

Julian's face went red. "No," he spluttered. "Not now, anyway."

"What does that mean?"

"We used to go out. That was a long time ago, though. Back in high school."

"Oh." I was happy and disappointed. So, they weren't together, but they used to be an item. I wondered if he still liked her. He had been spending a lot of time with her while completely ignoring me. I felt bad for feeling this way, but I couldn't help it.

Julian must have sensed my discomfort. "Are you okay?"

"Yes," I responded quickly. "I just didn't realise you were so close with her. There's a lot going on."

"She doesn't really have anyone else she can rely on."

"That's rough. I hope she'll be okay."

"I'll make sure of it."

As soon as I finished my coffee, I stood up. "I should get going."

Julian checked his watch. "So soon?"

"My next exam is tomorrow, so I'd like to study."

"Oh. Do you want a ride home?"

I shook my head. "It's okay. I'll walk."

Mock exams continued as if the whole fainting incident had never occurred. I tried my best to go on, putting everything behind me.

Lana is safe and resting now, I reminded myself.

I finished my last paper on Friday morning. With a full stop at the end of the concluding paragraph, I felt immense relief rush over me.

My number one priority during the holidays was to spend as much time as possible with Lana. I wanted to keep her spirits up.

"You're looking much better today," I said on my third visit.

"Really?" Lana asked, incredulous.

"Absolutely. I'm sure you'll be back to your old self in no time."

Lana bit her lip. I could tell she was holding something back.

"What's up?" I asked, eyes narrowed in suspicion.

Lana exhaled and went to her bedside drawers. She opened the top drawer and removed an envelope.

"What's that?"

"It's a letter from the Carrington Medical Society. I applied for a scholarship with them earlier this year. I had a phone interview a couple weeks ago."

"So, that's your acceptance letter?"

"Or rejection. I don't know. I haven't opened it yet."

"What are you waiting for?"

"I'm too nervous."

"Pass it here, then."

Lana hesitated but then passed it to me. She squeezed her eyes tight shut as I ran my finger under the seal. I carefully removed the letter, which was printed on heavy stock, and unfolded it.

Lana cracked open one eye and then swiftly shut it again. "What does it say?"

I cleared my throat and began. *"Dear, Lana Wu. Congratulations."*

Before I could continue, Lana burst into a cheer. We flung ourselves down on the bed. We lay on our backs, and I held up the letter and continued to read it. Lana's eyes followed as I read.

"We are pleased to provisionally award you the 2010 scholarship for Academic excellence."

"Provisionally?"

"I'm sure that's standard." I scanned the letter. "Here, you need to be accepted into a medical science degree, starting next year, and pass NCEA level three with excellence. Otherwise, the next eligible person on the wait list will be awarded the scholarship."

"That's it?"

"Yup. That shouldn't be a problem for you."

"I hope not. As long as I recover in time to give the final exams my all."

"I know you will."

Lana stretched out. "I'm so happy!"

"What does the scholarship cover?"

"Course fees for the first three years of my study."

"Wow, that's fantastic!"

"Yeah. There will still be a lot of other expenses. Living costs, course materials…"

"But there are still other scholarships you might be able to get?"

Lana nodded. "None as big as this, but they would definitely help."

"I'm so happy for you!" I rolled over and gave her a hug. As I pulled away, I couldn't help feeling Lana had everything much more sorted out than me. I tried not to let my feelings show.

"I wish we could go out to celebrate, but I'm still not supposed to leave the house," Lana said.

"We can celebrate once you're well enough."

"You better not forget."

"I won't. Are your parents at work? You should let them know. They'll be thrilled."

"You're right. Give me a moment. I'll call them."

I followed Lana to the living room and waited on the couch while she phoned her parents—her mother first and then her father—to relay the good news.

"Mum's going to make my favourite dumplings tonight," Lana said, dropping onto the couch beside me after her phone calls. "Today is a good day."

"Everything seems to be working out."

Lana nodded.

"I hope everything works out for me too," I murmured, not intending to sound envious.

"There couldn't be anyone more deserving than you," Lana said, and she sounded sincere. "Is everything going okay with Julian?"

"We've been texting pretty regularly now."

"Have you seen him again?"

"Not since we met up at the park. Now that he has turned in his portfolio, he has taken on more work at the bookstore. So, he's been busy with that. He's also still devoting a lot of his time to Charlotte since she's back in town."

"So, he has been seeing Charlotte a lot?"

I nodded. "He told me they're just friends, but…"

"Perhaps he's just a nice guy, looking out for his friend?"

"Yeah, perhaps. Or maybe he still has feelings for her."

"I hope that's not the case."

"Me too."

I brushed it from my mind, changing the subject. "Mock exam results come out next week."

Lana nodded.

"I think I did okay," I mused.

"Since I missed the exams, my results will probably be based on my work during the year. I hope I don't get judged too harshly."

"You'll definitely get excellence."

"I hope so."

I left Lana's house late in the afternoon and checked my phone as I walked home. Alarm set in when I saw three missed calls from Julian and an unopened text message. I read the message.

I have some news. Call me.

26

I stopped in my tracks and called Julian right away. My level of anxiety increased with each ring.

"Hi," he answered at last. His steady voice didn't give anything away.

"Sorry I missed your calls. What's up?"

He paused for effect before saying, "I've been accepted into Alberto Barsetti's atelier."

The first thought to enter my head was the fact he would be leaving. I refused to let my voice betray my disappointment. "That's fantastic. When do you leave?"

"In two months."

"That soon?"

"Yes."

"Wow. Congratulations. That's amazing. I'm happy for you, really. I knew you would get in."

"Thanks. Priscilla's going to throw me a party. A celebration of me getting into the atelier. Would you like to come? I mean..." he cleared his throat. "I'd like you to be there."

"Of course I'll come."

"Lana can come too if she's up to it. It's at Priscilla's house, next Friday. I'll let you know the address."

"Great, see you then."

After hearing Lana's and Julian's good news, I felt drained. I should have been feeling on top of the world, yet I selfishly felt like I was getting left behind in the dust.

My alarm clock buzzed me awake for the first time in two weeks. I groaned but managed to force myself from my warm bed.

When I arrived at school, I was surprised to see Lana standing beneath the tree at the school gates. She looked calm and composed. Her face was fresh, her hair straight, and her uniform clean and pressed.

I ran up to her. "You're back!"

"The doctor gave me the all clear. I can go back to my normal life as long as I take it easy. No extra-curricular activities or work for me. Just school then home time."

"I think that's good. Now, you can just focus on school."

"Yeah. I need to make sure I secure that scholarship." Determination gleamed in her eyes.

I felt like I didn't have to worry about her anymore. She was going to be just fine. Instead, I turned my concerns to mock exam results. English was first up. Anticipation bubbled inside me. Lana sat beside me, all cool and relaxed, seeing as she pretty much knew she was guaranteed excellence.

Fortunately, Mr. Donaldson didn't muck around. He handed back our papers at the beginning of class. I flicked straight to the back page of each essay booklet in quick succession. Excellence. Excellence. Excellence. I felt very pleased with myself.

"You did it!" Lana said.

"I did, didn't I?" For the first time in a while I felt as though something had gone my way.

The rest of my exam results trickled in over the next couple of days. My grades were more mixed but were mostly Merit. One step up from just passing, but not quite at the top level. Not bad, but not great. Not academic scholarship quality results. That's for sure.

After school on Wednesday, Lana and I met up at a small, local bar to celebrate her scholarship. Mrs. Wu let her have an exception to the no going out rule. We were the only people at the bar since it was still early in the evening. We sipped cocktails before digging into a wood-fired pizza.

"Thanks for your support through all this," Lana said. "I'm not sure I could have recovered so quickly without you."

I shrugged. "What are friends for? You would have done the same for me."

Lana smiled.

"Do you think you could wrangle another night out?" I asked.

"What for?"

"I forgot to tell you. Priscilla is hosting a party for Julian since he was accepted to the atelier."

"Hmmm… I think parties are probably out of bounds for me right now. You should definitely still go, though!"

"I will. I couldn't possibly miss this."

"How long until Julian leaves?"

"Two months."

"And you still don't know how he feels?"

I shook my head.

"You should tell him you like him."

"Huh?"

"I mean, what have you got to lose? Even if he rejects you, he'll be gone soon anyway. And, if you don't ask, you might never know if he felt the same way about you."

The very thought of confessing my feelings to Julian made my face grow hot and break out in a sweat. Lana had a point, though. A very good point indeed.

"You could be right," I uttered at last.

"I am right."

"You usually are."

"Then it's agreed? You'll tell Julian how you feel about him."

If I agreed to this, I would be locked into doing it, and I wasn't sure if I were ready. Then again, perhaps this was the kick in the butt I needed. I had been tiptoeing around the situation for a long time without taking any action. I weighed the pros and cons in my mind. The pros easily outweighed the cons, yet it was still difficult to agree to it.

Lana must have picked up on my mental turmoil. "Come on, Ivy. I don't want you to miss your chance. You've got this. I know you do."

It was the final push I needed. "All right."

"You'll do it?"

I nodded. "At the party. On Friday."

Lana broke out into the widest grin I had ever seen. She flung her arms around me. "You won't regret this. I promise."

"I'll let you know how it goes."

"Give me the full run down as soon as you get home on Friday night. Not a single detail missed."

27

I drove up to the large, ramshackle villa and parked on the side of the street. The night was surprisingly calm and quiet, considering there was meant to be a party going on. Then again, I couldn't envisage Priscilla being one to hold loud, raucous parties.

Through the windows I could see the lights were on, but I couldn't detect any movement. I climbed the front steps and gently tapped on the door. No one came, so I turned the handle without meeting resistance. The door opened into a hallway. The house was exactly as I had imagined—teeming with art and artefacts.

Paintings covered the walls, and bookcases housed volume after volume. A dusty chandelier hung from the ceiling. I followed the gentle murmur of voices through a large Victorian-styled living room. A pair of French doors opened out onto a spacious backyard where a small gathering sat around a large table. Tea lights flickered in the gentle breeze, and soft piano music flowed from a stereo.

I approached the group. I recognised a few faces from the

exhibition. Others I didn't know, but they looked around Julian's age.

Some of his old friends, perhaps? My eyes went to Julian, sitting at the head of the table. Next to him was Charlotte, looking effortlessly beautiful with her large green eyes, porcelain skin and strawberry-blonde hair in a messy braid. On the other side of Julian was a young man I didn't recognise. I silently pulled out a chair and sat down. Julian caught my eye and gave me a slight smile of acknowledgement. I wondered how I was possibly going to get a moment alone with him tonight. Not to mention the sight of him there next to Charlotte was almost enough to put me off entirely.

A selection of elegant finger foods was spread on the table —various cold cuts, cheeses and sauces. I speared a meatball with a toothpick.

"Hey, I'm Aaron. How do you know Julian?" the young man seated next to me asked.

I finished my mouthful. "I've done a little modelling for him here and there. Are you a friend of his?"

The man nodded. "That's right. Known each other since the beginning of high school."

"So, you two are close?"

"Well, we were very close at school. It's hard to keep things the same when you're living in two different places. I'm going to university in Auckland. I only come home once a year. We catch up then, but it's not really enough."

"That's tough."

"What do you do? Are you a student?"

I nodded. "I'm still in high school."

"Oh? I thought you were older? What's Julian doing fraternising with a girl your age?" He laughed.

"I'm eighteen. Exams are just around the corner. I won't be a high school student much longer."

"You're right. You're only three years younger, then. That's not so bad."

I wondered exactly what he was implying. I felt someone approach me from behind. My eyes flashed to Julian's chair, which was empty.

"I see you've met my friend Aaron," Julian said, appearing beside me.

"Yes."

"I'm sorry, I should have introduced you to everyone. I suppose there isn't really anyone here you know."

"It's okay. I could see you were stuck in the middle of a conversation."

"Can I get you something? A glass of wine?"

"I'd better not. I'm driving."

"Lemonade? Orange juice?"

"Oh, a lemonade would be great. Thanks."

Julian poured me a glass. He returned to his seat when Priscilla swept outside and commanded everyone's attention. A deep hush fell over everyone.

"As we all know, we are gathered here today to celebrate Julian's acceptance into the atelier of Alberto Barsetti. Ever since he discovered Barsetti's art in the National Gallery, Julian has pursued the opportunity to study under him. Two months from now, Julian leaves for Florence to do just that."

Everyone gave a round of applause.

"Julian, it has been an honour to have you work from my premises and to watch your art progress. I wish you the best of luck for the future." She handed Julian a gift wrapped in gold paper and ribbons.

A look of surprise crossed his face as he accepted the gift. His smile made me feel all emotional.

Julian opened the present. Inside was a gorgeous large-format hardcover book. *The Art of Florence* was inscribed on the cover. He had a quick flip through the thick volume.

"Thank you, Priscilla. It's lovely." He kissed her on the cheek.

The lively chatter recommenced, and Priscilla fetched more food from the kitchen.

People began to get up from their seats and mingle more. I tried to make my way over to Julian, but he was already inundated with people trying to talk to him. I sat back down and nursed my drink at the table.

"Ivy Beckett?" a gruff voice asked from behind me.

I turned to see a blonde-haired man with striking blue eyes and grey stubble.

"Every bit as lovely as Julian's drawings," he extended his hand. "Woody Anderson."

"Oh, you're Julian's art teacher." I shook his hand.

"*Former* art teacher. Julian will soon be under the tutelage of Alberto Barsetti." Woody sat down beside me. "That young man has a bright future ahead of him."

"You think so?"

Woody nodded. "Under Barsetti's guidance, he's sure to find success."

"I'm happy for him."

"Me too. A little envious too. If only I'd had such an opportunity at his age. Still, it couldn't have been an easy task to get accepted."

"He worked hard."

"You helped too. An artist needs a muse."

"Muse?" I laughed.

"I'm serious. You inspired him a lot. I can see why."

I blushed, embarrassed.

"We artists are greatly attracted to beauty."

"Beauty is subjective."

"You're right," Woody conceded. "Despite our different art styles, it seems Julian and I have similar taste."

I scoffed. "I wouldn't know about Julian's taste."

Woody raised an eyebrow. "Really? I thought it was pretty clear from the feelings expressed in his work."

"What do you mean?"

"Maybe I should leave you to ask him."

I looked across to Julian. Less people surrounded him now. Even Charlotte was no longer clinging to his side. Perhaps this was my chance.

"It's been a pleasure to meet you, Ivy."

"You too."

Woody left me. Nerves undulated in my stomach, and I desperately needed to use the bathroom. Before I had any time to mentally prepare, Julian headed towards me.

"Hey," he said.

"Hey."

"What were you talking about with Woody?"

"*You*, actually."

He looked at me quizzically. "Really? I hope you only had good things to say."

"Well…"

"What is it?"

"Sorry, can we continue this later? I need to use the bathroom." It was no use, I had to go. I slipped away before he could protest.

In the house, I stumbled down a dark hall and managed to locate the bathroom. While I relieved myself, I tried to rehearse in my head what I would say to Julian. Next time, I wouldn't be caught off-guard. I went to wash my hands in the adjacent room. Through the partially open door I saw the light was on. I covertly pushed it open a smidgen more.

Charlotte, stood in front of the mirror, reapplying lip gloss. It struck me more than ever just how beautiful she was.

"You can come in," Charlotte said. "Enjoying the party?"

"Yes. I'm happy to see Julian in such good spirits."

"It's nice, isn't it?" She couldn't hide a hint of sadness in her voice.

"Are you and Julian close?"

"Of course. And you? Julian mentions you every now and then."

"He does?"

Charlotte nodded. "You helped him out a lot while I've been away. Thank you."

"Oh." *So, that's all she meant.* "That's okay."

"I know Julian really appreciated it." Charlotte slipped her lip gloss back into her makeup bag.

She was about to leave when I spoke up. There was just something I wanted to clear up before I confessed my feelings to Julian. "So, is there something between you and Julian?" I asked. "I don't mean to pry or anything. It's just that I thought you looked like a couple."

Charlotte was rendered silent for a moment. It looked as if she were deciding something. Then, she uttered a single word.

"Yes."

28

My world came crumbling down. Charlotte's face flashed with a look of…regret? Guilt?

"I'm… sorry," I said, before I swiftly made my exit.

Back outside, I desperately tried to recompose myself. My efforts were futile. Seeing Julian at the table, smiling and laughing, was a sledgehammer to my heart. I realised just how strong my feelings were for him now. I wouldn't be able to make it to the end of the party without breaking down. I gathered my things in preparation for a sly exit, but Julian looked my way and must have noticed my distress. He was by my side at once.

"Ivy? Are you okay?"

"I just… I don't feel well."

"Can I get you anything? A glass of water? Paracetamol?"

"No, thanks." His kindness was almost unbearable. "I think I'll head home."

"Please…*stay*."

I was about to cry. "I want to go home."

Julian looked concerned, but he didn't push any further. "Will you be okay?"

I nodded. He handed me my coat.

Confused and upset, I drove home. As soon as I arrived, I headed straight to my room, slumped on the bed and cried into my pillow.

So, there was something between Julian and Charlotte after all. Of course, there was. *Why am I such an idiot?*

I slept fitfully. My phone went off several times during the night, but I ignored it, too exhausted to care.

When I woke late in the morning, it took a few moments for my memories to return. With bleary eyes, I reached for my phone. There were five new messages. The first four were from Lana.

So how did it go?

Are you home yet? What happened?

Ivy? You promised you'd tell me everything.

Is everything okay? Let me know in the morning.

The fifth message was from Julian.

Hope you are okay?

I'm not okay, I thought but texted back the opposite.

It took a huge amount of effort to drag myself to school on Monday. When I arrived, Lana rushed to my side. She looked pained.

"I'm so sorry," she said, pulling me into a hug.

"It's not your fault," I protested, my voice hoarse from a day of crying.

"I encouraged you to do this."

"It was the right thing to do."

"I never imagined it would turn out this way."

"It was a shock for me too."

Lana sighed. "At least you know now."

I forced a smile. "Yeah. Now, I won't be so sad about him leaving. I can focus on my future."

"That's a good way to look at it." Lana fiddled with her jersey hem. She seemed preoccupied.

"What's wrong?"

She frowned. "I just can't shake the feeling something doesn't add up."

"What do you mean?"

"You said Julian's art teacher seemed convinced Julian liked you."

"That's right."

"And Julian's friend joked about your age difference."

"Yeah. Now, that you mention it, that was pretty strange."

Lana paced in thought before coming to a pause. She looked me in the eye. "Do you think we can trust Charlotte?"

My thoughts plunged back to my conversation with Julian in the park. *"She seems to have it all together… She's in a downward spiral… She's depressed…"* Charlotte wasn't stable, according to him.

But still. What reason could she possibly have to deceive me?

"I don't think she would lie about something like this."

"I suppose so." Lana chewed her lip. "It was just a thought."

We didn't have time to ruminate any further. We headed to class.

I was too mentally exhausted to function for most of the day. The events of the night of the party replayed over and over in my head. By fifth period, I had a pounding headache. When class was finally dismissed I exhaled in relief.

As I walked home from school, Lana's comment about Charlotte resurfaced at the forefront of my mind. A tantalising shred of hope, but I refused to let myself cling to it. I wasn't going to open myself up to more hurt. I had to get over this.

On my way up the driveway, I absentmindedly checked the letter box. I sorted through the mail and stopped when I found something addressed to me. I turned over the envelope. Stamped on the back was *The Elias Institute.*

29

I clutched the envelope in my trembling hands. I felt so dizzy, I could've fainted. Gathering myself, I brought the mail inside. I took the letter to the living room where I sat down on the couch. Several minutes passed before I worked up the courage to open it. I held my breath while I gently tore the seal open. I pulled out the sheet inside and unfolded it.

Dear Ivy Beckett,

Thank you for your application to the creative writing course at the Elias Institute. We regret to inform you that your application has been unsuccessful.

I couldn't read any more. My eyes welled up. My breath caught in my throat. I choked. Then, I sobbed hysterically. Just like that, my dreams had been shattered. Everything had been for nothing.

How could I have been so stupid? Of course, I was never going to get in. These thoughts swirled in my head, taunting me. I curled into a ball and cried my heart out. I stayed like that until Mum came home from work. She found me in a quivering heap on the couch, my eyes swollen and red. The letter was screwed up in the middle of floor.

"Ivy, what on earth happened?"

I tried to speak but couldn't.

Mum picked up the letter, smoothed it out and read it, her expression turning into a grimace. "I see," she said. She reached out to me and wrapped me in her arms.

I sobbed against her chest.

Mum rocked me until I stopped crying. "Everything will be okay," she said, but everything was not okay.

Julian liked Charlotte, not me, and I wasn't good enough to get into my dream school.

"There's always law school, honey. I'm sure you'll get in."

This made my wails start all over again.

Mum hushed me. "I'm sorry. I know how much you wanted this."

Tears rolled down my cheeks. Mum held me as I cried.

When Dad got home, he quietly watched the scene before him.

"I've got this," Mum said.

Dad nodded. "I'll make dinner."

While Dad cooked, Mum took me to the bathroom and ran me a bath. I got in and tried to relax. The hot water soothed my aching body, but my eyes still stung with the remnants of my tears.

I walked through the next few days completely numb to everything. Even Lana couldn't get through to me. She had been researching other creative writing courses but couldn't find anything. Application deadlines had closed long ago.

Another letter arrived for me. The envelope had the Hill University logo on it. I didn't care at all. Whether I got in or not, nothing could be any worse than the current situation I was in. I left the unopened envelope on the kitchen counter.

Mum came to my room that evening. "Your letter from Law School is here!"

"Oh, I didn't see it." I was less than enthused but tried not to show it.

"Do you want to open it?"

"You can do it. I don't want another shock."

Mum put her reading glasses on and sat down on the edge of the bed. She opened the envelope. Her eyes quickly scanned the letter. Her smile said it all.

"You've done it! You're in!" She stood up, grabbed my hand and pulled me towards her. "I knew you would. This is what you were meant to do."

"I guess you're right," I conceded with a sigh.

"So, you'll accept?" Mum asked, her hands clasped together as if praying.

"I will."

Mum hugged me.

Later that night, I watched as she filled out the form, confirming my place. All that was left to do was mail it back, along with the required acceptance fee. Then, my future would be locked in.

30

The bell rang at the end of English class. I put my books away. "Ivy, can I have a word with you?" Mr. Donaldson asked.

"Uh, sure."

He waited until everyone else had left the room before pulling out a chair opposite me. "I heard the acceptance letters for Elias had gone out. How did you do?"

I looked down at my feet. "I didn't get in."

"Oh, dear. I was sure you would get in. They must have had a very high quality of applicants this year."

I could tell he was just trying to cheer me up.

"Did you apply anywhere else?"

"The law degree at Hill."

"Any other creative writing courses?"

I shook my head. "I got into law school."

"Will you accept it?"

"Yes."

Mr. Donaldson furrowed his brow. "I thought you changed your mind about being a lawyer?"

I shrugged. "Maybe this is the path for me. I'm not a very good writer, but maybe I'll make a good lawyer. I won't know unless I try."

"It's a big investment, Ivy. In both time and money. You should be sure this is what you want to do."

"What other option do I have?"

"There are so many options."

"What options?"

"A university education isn't the be all and end all. You don't need a degree to be a writer."

I let his words sink in. "I guess so."

"There's travel, work, volunteering, starting a business... The world is full of possibilities for a young person such as yourself."

"I didn't really think about anything like that."

"Give it some more thought before you commit to university. How long do you have to accept your place at law school?"

"Around three weeks, I think."

"Then there's no point rushing into it."

"No. I suppose not."

"Chin up, Ivy. I'm sure things will work out for you. Whatever path you choose."

"Thank you, Mr. Donaldson."

I really took his words to heart. It was true. I hadn't given much thought to other options. Throughout my whole life it just seemed like a given that I would finish high school then go to university. Anything else was for slackers. Perhaps I had been wrong. Could there possibly be another path for me?

When I got home from school, I went to my room. The acceptance form to Law School had vanished from my desk. I wondered if Mum had posted it already. I prayed she hadn't.

When Mum arrived home, I approached her. "Did you send back my acceptance form?" I asked, abruptly.

"No, I didn't have time today. It's in my bag."

A sense of relief flooded me, but it didn't make the next words any easier. I took in a breath. "Good. Don't send it." I braced myself for her reaction.

"Why? Did you forget something?"

"No."

Mum's face turned pale.

"I'm not sure I want to go," I continued, "I want to give it more thought."

"But you seemed so sure the other day," Mum spluttered.

"Well, I've changed my mind."

"This isn't about this writing nonsense again is it?"

"So, what if it is? And it isn't nonsense."

"Oh, *grow up*, Ivy. Creative writing isn't a real career. How do you expect to succeed when you couldn't even get into Elias?"

Her words stung. "I'm not listening to this."

"Tough luck. I'm sending the acceptance form tomorrow. You'll thank me later."

"Bitch." I said under my breath.

"What did you say?"

"Bitch!" I yelled.

I strode out of the house and slammed the door in her face before she could respond. Tears in my eyes, I ran down the driveway. When I was far away from the house I slowed down but continued aimlessly. Even as it began to grow dark I kept walking. The street lights flicked on. I realised I was walking to Opulence. Adrenaline surged through me. My sadness gave way to anger. Anger gave way to resolve. I'm not going to law school, I decided. I didn't want to do anything that would please her. I only wanted to please myself.

When I finally arrived at the small block of shops, all was quiet and dark. I clung to the tiniest kernel of hope that Priscilla, or even Julian, would be in the shop. The door was locked. I knocked and prayed. Finally, after a rustling sound, the door opened.

"My dear," Priscilla exclaimed.

I fell into her arms. The familiar scent of her perfume comforted me.

"Whatever is the matter?"

"Everything's messed up."

"Sounds like you had better come in. Let's have something to eat and a chat."

Priscilla led me inside. The shop was illuminated by a single lamp at the counter, where piles of paper were stacked and spilling over.

"I didn't think you would be here," I said.

"You're in luck. I needed to get some paperwork done tonight, so I'm staying late."

We went to the kitchen. The smell of Chinese food flooded my nostrils.

"Lucky I ordered extra. I thought Julian might come by." Priscilla served me a plate of fried rice and sweet and sour pork.

"Thank you," I said, before greedily digging in. I hadn't realised quite how hungry I was.

Priscilla waited patiently as I ate.

When I was ready, I explained my situation. "I didn't get into the creative writing course I applied to."

"I see."

"And I didn't apply for any other back-up options. Only law school."

Priscilla waited for me to continue.

"I got into law school, but I can't face going there. It's not what I want. I had a huge fight with my mum over it."

"Ivy, let me tell you a story about a young woman."

I wondered where this was going.

"She graduated high school. Everyone told her she was intelligent and had a bright future ahead of her. Her parents wanted her to do well. She went to university to study to be a dentist. After three years of studying dental surgery, she could no longer deny her feelings. It wasn't for her, so she quit. She spent the next year unemployed, trying to figure out what to do with her life."

I grimaced. This story wasn't making me feel any better.

"One day, it dawned on her. She had a fascination with art. So why not learn more about it? She decided to go back to school to study art history. Her parents thought she was crazy, but their opinion no longer held any sway. She ended up getting a part-time job at an auction house. She then went on to get a master's degree, travel the world, and finally, open her own shop."

I realised, perhaps a little late, she was talking about herself.

"My point is that life isn't straightforward. There are many twists and turns."

"I know. But I feel so disorientated."

"That's only natural."

"What should I do?"

"I can't tell you what's in your heart. You'll have to work that out yourself."

"My heart tells me to be a writer. I'd like to write a novel."

"Then write that novel. All you need to do is choose a lifestyle which will enable it."

She made it sound so simple. Perhaps it really was simple. I felt a weight lift from my shoulders. "Thank you, Priscilla. I feel a lot better."

"You're welcome, Ivy. You can always talk to me."

A smile spread across my face. "I can't believe you originally wanted to be a dentist."

"I can barely believe it myself. It feels like a lifetime ago."

Hours had passed since I ran away from home. I wondered if my parents were beginning to worry about me. Nevertheless, I couldn't face going back. Not yet.

"Stay as long as you like," Priscilla said. "I have work to do, but you're free to stay here. Or you could go upstairs."

"The studio."

Priscilla nodded. "Although it's not much of a studio now. It's mostly been cleared out."

"Julian isn't using it anymore?"

"He's getting ready to leave. Most of his things have already been sold or packed up."

"I see."

"Head on up. I'll be down here if you need me."

The narrow staircase creaked as I ascended. In the studio, I flicked on the light. The room was now completely empty except for the desk in front of the window, cleared of all the mess.

"It's like he's already left," I said to myself, an unexpected note of melancholy in my voice.

I sat at the desk and gazed out over the township below.

Many minutes passed while I was lost in thought. I had so

much to think about. My life was now a blank slate. Anything was possible. The thought was thrilling and terrifying.

Footsteps approached.

"Ivy?"

The voice startled me. Priscilla hadn't come to check up on me as I'd thought. It was Julian.

31

My heart hammered in my chest. I stood up and faced Julian. He was dressed smartly as if he had just been out somewhere nice. Had he been out on a date? With Charlotte, perhaps. I could smell the faintest trace of alcohol on him.

He stared at me searchingly with his green eyes. Those large, intense, dreamy eyes.

"Priscilla told me you were up here."

"Did she tell you what happened?"

"No. Just that you were upset and you're gonna stay here for a while."

"Oh! I think I ate your food."

Julian grinned. "That's okay. I've already eaten."

"Have you just been out somewhere?"

He nodded. "Farewell drinks with my art class."

"That's nice."

"Are you all right?"

"I just had a big fight with my mum. I'm feeling better now, but I really don't want to go home."

"You could stay the night at my place." Julian blushed, probably just realising what he had said. "Or Priscilla's. I'm sure she wouldn't mind."

"Thanks for the offer, but I'd better not. I have school tomorrow and I can't just show up in these clothes. My uniform is at home."

"I suppose it's for the best. You can't avoid your parents forever. It's better to resolve it now."

I nodded.

"Well, if there's anything I can help you with, just let me know."

Tell him. Tell him how you feel. The voice in my head urged me to take action. The words were on the tip of my tongue. My heart raced.

"I guess I'll see you around." He turned and headed back towards the door.

The words escaped my mouth. "Please don't go."

He stopped in his tracks and turned around, looking at me inquisitively.

"This could be the last time we see each other."

"It could?" Julian asked softly. "I hope not."

His sincerity made my heart melt. Words escaped me. I gathered myself and tried again.

"I like you." *There.* I nervously awaited his reaction.

He did not speak. I couldn't read his expression. My hopes diminished by the second. I was in agony before he took one step towards me and then another. His intention was now clearly written on his face. Eyes trained upon my lips, he approached. In one swift movement, he lifted my chin and pressed his lips to mine.

He pulled away suddenly. "I'm sorry."

"What for?"

"I couldn't resist."

"I didn't want you to."

"Ivy, I can't be with you."

"Is it Charlotte?"

"What?"

"She told me there was something going on between you two."

"She did?" Julian looked genuinely flummoxed.

"Yes. She did."

"Well, now I'm pissed off at myself for giving her that impression." He rubbed his temples. "I have only ever been interested in you."

"Then why can't you be with me?"

"I don't want to hurt you. I'm moving away. And not for the short-term."

"I know that."

"I don't want to start something with you just to have it cut short."

"But, surely, being together for a short while is better than not being together at all? We don't even have to be boyfriend and girlfriend."

"Then what are we?"

"Just two people who like each other and who want to make the most of the time they have left together." I could tell I was wearing his resistance down.

"Are you sure you know what you're asking for?"

"Yes. I'm sure."

"Okay, then." He pulled me tightly against him. "I'm not going to hold back," he murmured against the crook of my neck.

His breath made my skin prickle. He kissed my neck, my cheek and my lips. With shaking breath, he made out with me.

When he finally pulled away, his voice sounded ragged. "My offer still stands. Stay the night with me."

His forwardness took me by surprise. Apart from a few awkward kisses, I was not very experienced with guys. Luckily there was no need to think it over. I couldn't with school the next day.

"I can't."

"Oh, that's right. Sorry."

"I should probably go home now. I've been out for hours." Nothing could spoil my mood now, not even having to face Mum.

"I'm sure Priscilla would give you a lift. I need one too."

We went downstairs. Priscilla looked up from her work. She smiled knowingly but didn't say anything.

I crept in through the front door. My parents were in the living room, watching television. They didn't look in my direction. I tiptoed to my room. Closing the door behind me, I sighed with relief. My thoughts immediately turned to Julian and the scene that had just unfolded.

Julian. I hugged my pillow tight against me.

A firm knock on my door snapped me from my fantasies. I ignored it, hoping to be left alone. The door opened anyway. Dad stood there, the vein on his forehead throbbing. He looked angrier than I had ever seen him.

32

Dad's eyes blazed. I gulped.

"Don't you ever leave the house at night without telling us where you're going," he yelled.

"I'm sorry," I whimpered, holding up the duvet like a shield.

Dad's breathing slowed. He softened. "Do you have any idea how worried we were about you?"

I didn't reply.

"If anything happened to you…"

"I'm fine."

"We know you've been feeling down lately."

"I was upset."

"I don't like seeing you like this."

"Everything's okay now," I assured him.

Dad hugged me. "Would you tell me if anything's bothering you?"

"Yes, Dad."

"I love you."

"I love you, too."

He stood up, arms crossed. "Tomorrow night, let's have a family meeting. We need to clear the air."

I nodded.

"Oh, and your mother wants a word with you."

I groaned, but decided it was better to get it over with. "Bring her in."

Dad left. I waited tensely as Mum's footsteps approached, wondering what she had in store for me. I braced myself as she entered the room.

Her posture was crumpled, and her eyes were bloodshot. Something in her had changed. My tension drained.

"Ivy, I want to apologise." Her voice cracked. "What I said before… I crossed the line."

Tears welled up in my eyes.

"It's just hard for me to accept that you want something different than what I want. We were on the same page for so long…"

I swallowed, my throat dry. "I know, but I can't change the way I feel."

Mum sat on the bed and cradled me in her arms like she used to do when I was a child. "It's all right," she said softly. "I don't blame you. You've done nothing wrong. It's me who has been at fault. In the end, I just want you to be happy. That's the main thing. Somewhere along the line, I lost sight of that."

I sniffled, my bottom lip trembling.

Mum pulled an envelope from her pocket and handed it to me. The acceptance form to Law School. "I think you should keep this. It's your decision whether or not it should be sent, not mine."

~

The next morning, Dad called a family meeting. We sat around the dining room table.

"Ivy, we want to know what's going on. Have you made a decision about next year yet?" Dad asked.

I took a deep breath before letting the words I had rehearsed fall out. "I don't want to accept my place at law school. It's not the life for me. If you send me there, it will be a waste of your money."

My parents didn't make any attempt to argue. Dad listened calmly, and Mum sat in silence, arms crossed.

"So, it's settled," Dad said. "Law school is off the table."

I felt relieved.

"What will you do instead?" Mum asked. "It's too late to apply anywhere else for next semester."

"I won't go to university," I replied coolly.

"Then what will you do? Bumming around at home isn't an option."

"I know that! I'll get a job."

"Without any qualifications you won't be able to get anything better than minimum wage."

"I'll find something."

"There's one more thing. We've decided you can't stay here. In the real world, people pay rent and bills. You need to learn what that's like."

I looked to Dad.

"Sorry, Ivy. I know it's harsh, but we think it's for the best. We want you to figure out how to support yourself instead of relying on us. You can stay here until the end of February. That's when you would have left for university."

"Fine. I can look after myself."

"Good. So, it's agreed. If Ivy turns down her place at law

school, she must sort out a job, and leave home by the end of February."

A harsh blow, but not exactly unexpected. I was never going to be able to live by my own rules while living under the same roof anyway. It was better this way. Finally, I would have my freedom.

Lana shrieked with utter glee when I told her the news.

"I can't believe it! He's liked you this whole time? What about Charlotte? Was he a good kisser?"

"He didn't like Charlotte. He liked me. And, yes, he is an amazing kisser."

My cell phone vibrated in my skirt pocket. Who would be calling me at a time like this? I got a shock when I saw it was Julian.

"He's calling you!" Lana said. "What are you waiting for? Answer it!"

I accepted the call. Lana listened over my shoulder.

"Hey, it's me," Julian said, his voice all raspy and sexy.

"Hey," I squeaked.

"I just wanted to say sorry about last night."

"What do you mean?"

"I was a bit drunk. I don't know if you could tell."

Had he really been that drunk? What if it was all just a drunken mistake, then? My mind rushed to all sorts of conclusions.

Please no.

"Do you regret what happened?"

"No. Not at all."

Whew.

"Except when I asked you back to my place. I shouldn't have put you on the spot like that. I just got a bit over excited."

"Excited?"

"*Well…*"

"Oh!" I couldn't help but let out a giggle.

Lana managed to bite her tongue.

"So, uh, what are you doing Saturday night?"

"No plans."

"Do you want to go out with me?"

"A date?"

"Yes. A date."

"I would love to. Did you have something in mind?"

"Yes. The symphony orchestra is in town. I booked tickets ages ago. I was going to take Priscilla, but I don't think she'd mind if I invited you instead."

"Are you sure?"

"Absolutely."

"Okay, then. Let's go."

"All right. I'll pick you up on Saturday."

33

Every few minutes, I found myself glancing at the clock, but it seemed as if time stood still. The anticipation of the evening's date was killing me. I tried to study, but I couldn't concentrate. I tried to watch a movie, but I couldn't follow the plot. My mind kept wandering, daydreaming about what might happen on the date with Julian.

Will he kiss me again? Will he try to hold my hand? My thoughts continued like that until it was time to start getting ready.

I picked a dress and did my makeup. Satisfied with my appearance, I waited in the living room, idly flicking through a magazine. I almost jumped out of my skin when there was a knock at the door. Julian stood on the doorstep, looking utterly handsome and dreamy in black jeans and a button-up shirt.

"H-hey," I stuttered.

Julian surveyed me, his mouth dropping. "You look…"

"Nice?"

He shook his head. "*Exquisite.*"

"Thanks." I tucked a loose strand of hair behind my ear.

"That's the first time I've been described that way, but I could get used to it."

Julian laughed. "Good. You'll be hearing that a lot."

I smiled sheepishly.

A fine mist of rain in the air dusted Julian's hair with tiny droplets. He brushed them away. "Come on, let's go," he said.

I followed him to the car he had borrowed from Priscilla for the night.

"What symphony are they playing?" I asked, getting into the car.

"Tchaikovsky's symphony number six. *The Passionate Symphony*."

"I'm not familiar with it. I don't know much about classical music."

Julian grinned. "You're in for a treat."

We drove to the theatre in town—a grand and magnificent but run-down building in major need of renovation. I liked it, though. It had character. The interior looked like an Arabic palace with arched doorways and intricate geometric patterns on the walls.

We passed the crowd in the foyer and headed straight up the stairs. Julian led me to our seats, which were located in the front row of the circle.

"Wow. We have a perfect view," I said in awe, looking out over the stage.

"Yeah. These seats are the best," Julian said.

I made myself comfortable on the worn, red velvet seat. The theatre was still mostly empty.

"Looking forward to the concert?" Julian asked.

"Yes. I've never been to see an orchestra play before."

"That's a shame."

"Do you come often?"

Julian shook his head. "Not anymore. My parents used to take me a lot, though. They wanted to make my brothers and me form an appreciation for the arts. We were always going to the ballet, the opera, the orchestra, plays… I was really into it. My brothers, not so much, but they didn't mind it either."

"You were lucky to have parents like that."

"Yeah. I have to keep reminding myself that my upbringing wasn't exactly normal."

"Do you think their influence made you decide to be an artist?"

"No. I like to think I would've been an artist no matter what. My parents just helped me get to where I am."

"That's a good way to look at it."

The theatre was filling up and the orchestra and conductor took their place on stage. A deep hush fell over the audience. Barely audible above a low rumble, the music began, led by the bassoon. Slowly, strings joined in and then clarinets. The music built and built. I was enthralled.

Next to me, it looked like Julian was in a trance. Completely immersed in the music, a serious expression on his face. His eyebrows were animated with emotion. I grinned, enamoured with his cuteness.

My attention returned to the orchestra, and I felt myself fall into that same trance-like state.

Powerful strings opened the heart-rending fourth movement. The music grew darker, sadder. Drums pounded, leading into the finale. On a note of hopelessness, the music faded. Silence all around. The conductor bowed in a grand sweep and applause broke out.

"That was incredible!" I exclaimed as we left the theatre.

Julian nodded. "It was. I'm glad you enjoyed it."

"I wished it would never end."

"What time are your parents expecting you back?"

"I have to be home by ten."

Julian checked his watch. "We've still got plenty of time. There's a park not too far from here. Let's go for a walk."

"Good idea."

Julian guided the way to the nearby park. Dense blossoming trees and lush foliage surrounded us. Silver moonlight rippled on a stream.

"It's beautiful. I've never come here at night before." I examined our surroundings in wonder.

"It's nice, isn't it? There's no one else here."

We came to a large fountain illuminated in sapphire-blue light.

"So pretty!" I took a closer look. Coins littered the bottom. "Have you ever made a wish at a fountain?"

"I don't think so."

"Let's try it." I searched my purse for change. "You first." I gave him a coin.

"Okay." Julian stepped up to the fountain. "I wish—"

"Don't say it aloud! It should be a secret."

Julian closed his eyes. He tossed the twenty-cent coin and it landed with a plop.

"So, what did you wish for?"

"I thought it was supposed to be a secret?"

"I know, but now I want to know!"

"Well, I'm not telling you."

I pouted.

My turn next. I stepped up, coin tight in my grip. Of all the things I could have wished for, that night, the only thing on my mind was Julian.

I wish we will end up together.

The coin left my grip, plunging to the bottom of the fountain. The night felt so magical, I let myself believe it would come true.

We continued deeper into the park.

Julian took in a breath.

"What are you thinking about?" I asked.

"My regrets."

"How can you think about that on a night like this?"

Julian frowned. "I told Charlotte you and I are together…"

"Oh. How did she take it?"

"She was surprised." He rubbed his forehead. "I can't blame her for thinking I liked her. I let her in. I let her lean on me while I pushed you away. No wonder you were both confused. I'm sorry."

"It's okay," I assured him. "I forgive you."

"I just want to make it up to you."

"This night has more than made up for it."

Julian eased. "That's good."

In the centre of the park, a bridge stretched across the stream. As we crossed it Julian took my hand, entwining his fingers with mine. He rubbed his thumb over the back of my hand. His touch sent a jolt through me. Nervousness made my hand clammy. I hoped he didn't notice.

On the other side of the park, there was a playground. In my excitement, I broke away. "Let's go on the swings!"

I dashed over to the playground, Julian lagging behind me. We sat down on the swings. Ahead of us, the moon was full and breathtaking.

"I've had a wonderful time tonight," I said.

"Me too," Julian said.

The stars twinkled above us. I felt so happy. I swung higher and higher. Next to me, Julian sat, but did not swing.

"Don't you like it?" I asked.

"I get motion sickness."

"Is that so? How sad."

"I suppose it is." He chuckled.

I stopped swinging, gently coming back down. "When did you start liking me?" I asked, coyly.

Julian looked thoughtful. "I don't really know. It just snuck up on me."

"It wasn't love at first sight?" I asked, joking.

"Not quite." Julian laughed. "But I certainly took notice of you."

"Me too."

"I suppose I realised my feelings when you invited me to go away with you. It took me completely off-guard, but I knew straight away I wanted to go. I wanted to spend time with you."

"Did you think something might happen between us?"

"I wasn't sure, but I wanted something to happen."

"We almost kissed."

"I stopped myself. I felt like I was being reckless."

I bit my lip. "I like it when you're reckless."

"Ivy, come here."

I slid off the swing and approached him. He motioned for me to sit on his lap. I sat on his knee and he put his arms around me, pulling my head to his chest. I could smell his cologne, earthy and deep. He ran his hand through my hair and kissed me on the forehead. His lips were so soft. I couldn't help wanting more. I lifted my head and kissed him on the lips, gently at first, but then with growing passion. He didn't resist, kissing me deeper, feverishly.

Voices approached and we jolted apart.

34

A rowdy group of young teenagers headed towards us. They were smoking, drinking, and talking mainly in expletives.

"Did they see us?" I asked self-consciously, smoothing my ruffled hair.

"Who cares?" Julian said. He took my hand and led me away. "It's almost ten. Should I drop you home now?"

"Yes, please."

We walked back to the car, hand in hand.

"I had an amazing time tonight," I said.

"Me too. I hope we can go out again soon."

I nodded. "We need to make the most of the time we have left together."

"You're right. Every moment counts."

As we drove back to my house, it started to rain. Julian turned the wipers on. We sat in silence most of the way, listening to the raindrops on the roof of the car.

As we neared my house, Julian said, "I wasn't sure if I

should bring this up tonight, but I want to know. How are things going with your parents?"

"It's okay. We had a family meeting. I told them I'm not going to study law. They accepted my decision, even if they weren't too happy about it. They're not going to pressure me anymore."

"That's good."

"They want me to move out, though. They have given me until the end of February to sort myself out."

"That sucks. But still, I suppose it can't be helped."

"Yeah. Despite that, I feel a bit better about everything now."

"What about your grandparents? Have you spoken to them again since we left the lodge?"

"No. Why?"

"No reason. It just seemed like they really care for you. Maybe more than your parents do."

"You're right. And I miss them too. Perhaps I should give them a call?"

"That might be a good idea."

By the time we arrived at my house, it was after ten. The lights were on, so I knew my parents had waited up for me.

"Well, goodnight." I unbuckled my seatbelt.

"Can I have a goodnight kiss?" Julian asked.

I smiled, leaned over and gave him a kiss on the lips. Short and sweet.

"Goodnight, Julian."

"Goodnight, Ivy."

~

Even with final exams fast approaching, I spent every spare minute with Julian. My parents were starting to get concerned.

"I hope you're still going to take your exams seriously," Mum said.

"Don't worry. I'm staying in tonight to study."

"Good. Let me know if you need anything."

Although my future was no longer dependent on good exam results, I still wanted to do well. It was the least I could do after everything I'd put my parents through. I went to my room and settled in with a stack of textbooks and a notepad. Headphones on, I tried to focus on studying. Eventually, I got into the flow of it.

It didn't last long. I was snapped from my flow when my headphones were yanked off my head.

"Hey!"

"Phone for you," Mum said.

I took the phone and pressed it to my ear. "Hello?"

"Hello, Ivy. This is Catherine Hitchcock. I'm in charge of admissions to the Creative Writing programme at The Elias Institute."

My heart jumped.

"I just wanted to call regarding your application to the Elias Institute."

What could this possibly be about? My application was rejected, wasn't it?

"Have you received your letter?"

"Yes. I didn't get in."

"Yes. That's right. But I wanted to let you know the admissions team was impressed by your application."

"Oh?"

"Yes. You have a fresh voice, and we all enjoyed reading your work."

"Thank you."

"You're probably wondering why you weren't accepted. The truth is, we contemplated your application for a long time. Ultimately, we decided you weren't quite ready. We rarely take anyone straight out of high school. Most of our students are more mature. Life experience is really valuable for writers."

"That makes sense."

"You have talent, Ivy. That's clear. But you wouldn't be a good fit for this course. That is why you were passed up this time."

"I understand."

"Take my advice, Ivy. Get out there into the big, wide world. Write, study, work and travel. Experience what the world has to offer. Then, you will be ready to reapply to study here. We would gladly take you."

"Thanks for the advice. I'll keep that in mind."

"What are you doing next year?"

"I haven't quite sorted it out yet. The only thing I know is I want to write every day."

"Well, that's a good start. Good luck, Ivy."

"Thank you, Catherine."

"Hope to hear from you again in the future. Goodbye."

"Bye."

The conversation brought me a sense of closure, and I smiled. At least I knew why I didn't get in. It hadn't been a lack of talent. It had been a preference for more mature students. Why hadn't I thought of that before? It seemed obvious now. Of course, they would want students with life experience. I sighed.

I tried to get back into my study but couldn't concentrate. The daunting question of what I was going to do for the next year hovered over me. Although I had given it a lot of thought,

I had yet to come up with a satisfying resolution. Thoughts swirled around in my head, and I found it hard to get to sleep that night.

Trying to relax, I pictured myself at my grandparents' lodge, taking a walk in the countryside. I thought about the encounter with Julian—when we almost kissed. I remembered helping my grandfather in the garden. A deep sense of calm enveloped me, and I drifted off.

When I awoke, it struck me. I knew a place I could live, a place I could work, a sanctuary where I could practice my writing. The answer had been so simple all along.

35

Here goes. I picked up the phone. My hand trembled. I had never been so nervous about calling my grandparents. But this call was so important. It would determine everything. I dialled the lodge, growing more tense with each ring.

Finally, my grandfather answered. "Hello?"

"It's me, Ivy."

"Ivy? What a pleasant surprise. How are you?"

I immediately felt calmer upon hearing his voice. Grandpa would always try to do best by me, I knew that. He was a sweet and caring man. I opened up to him.

"Actually, I'm in a predicament."

"A predicament you say? Can I help?"

"Yes. I think you can. That's why I'm calling."

"I'm all ears."

"Long story short, I need work and a place to live."

"My goodness, that is a predicament."

"You know how you were thinking about getting someone to help out at the lodge? Someone to live on site and take care of maintenance tasks...?"

"I remember."

"Has that position been filled?"

"No. Not yet. It was just an idea at this stage, so we haven't started looking for anyone."

"Well, if you're still considering it, I would like to have a go at it."

"Well, this is a shock! What about your plans to go to university?"

"That didn't work out. I didn't get into the creative writing programme. I got into law, but I've decided I just can't stomach it. It's not for me."

"Well, it's better to decide now than part way through."

"Yeah, that's what I thought. Anyway, my parents won't let me keep living here. So, I want to get a job."

"Are you sure doing maintenance work would make you happy?"

"I love the lodge, you know I do. I enjoyed helping you out when I visited. Working there would be refreshing. And I could write in my spare time. I'm hoping to complete a novel."

"That's very ambitious." Grandpa sounded in good spirits.

"It wouldn't be forever, just until I decide what to do next. I might reapply to study creative writing the next year, or maybe I'll do some travelling."

"Well, I can't make any promises at this stage, but I'll discuss it with your grandmother and we'll make a decision."

"Thank you!"

"Bye, Ivy. We'll call you back."

I was nervous, but Grandpa had sounded excited by the idea. I didn't think Grandma would be against it either.

Fortunately, I wasn't left hanging for long. Grandma called me within an hour.

"Ivy, I would love it if you came to live with us! What a brilliant idea!" she said with vast enthusiasm.

"I would earn my place of course, working on the property."

"Of course, you will, dear. You've always been a big help whenever you've visited. This is going to be great."

"So, it's a deal, then?"

"It's a deal. When will you come?"

"Would February be okay?"

"That soon? We need to start making preparations."

"I'm looking forward to it."

"You're a hard worker, Ivy. I know everything will work out."

"I feel so relieved now."

"Only too glad to help, my dear."

I felt so light, so free. Everything that had been weighing me down had been shifted. Living and working at the lodge would be the perfect lifestyle for me as I worked on my novel.

My parents were in the living room when I made my announcement. "I'm moving in with my grandparents. I'm going to work at the lodge."

"What's that, honey?" Dad asked, eyebrows raised.

"I've just been on the phone with them. It's all arranged."

"And they're okay with this?"

I nodded. "They're completely on board with it."

He stood up. "Is this what you want?"

"Yes."

"Then I support you." He hugged me. "I'm glad you figured something out. My parents will be happy to have you around."

"Thanks, Dad."

"What are your thoughts, dear?" he asked Mum.

Mum put aside the magazine she was reading. "I think it's a good idea as long as you make yourself useful and not a burden."

"Of course, I will."

"When will you go?" Dad asked.

"I don't know yet, but I'll be out of your hair by the end of February as promised."

"No rush, honey. Take your time."

Mum nodded. "End of February was just a guideline."

"Thanks, but I hope to leave as soon as possible. As soon as Grandma and Grandpa are prepared to take me."

"We'll miss you," Dad said, almost tearing up. "We'll visit you as much as we can."

"Thanks. I'd like that."

After informing my parents, I was desperate to tell Julian. I texted him.

I have news.

I met Julian at the waterfront. He stood, windswept, leaning against the fence. I rushed over and flung my arms around him, almost knocking him off his feet.

"I did it!"

Julian grinned, amused. "You did what?"

"I know what I'm going to do next year."

I relayed my news to him as we walked side by side down the boardwalk.

"That sounds perfect. I think it will work well for you," Julian said.

"Me too. I can't wait to move there."

"When do you leave?"

"Sometime in February."

"So, you still have a few months to prepare."

"Yeah. It will probably go fast, though."

"Do you have a job lined up for the summer holidays?"

"No. If I can't find anything, I'll just relax and take it easy."

"I can put a word in for you at Lucky Books, if you like."

"Really? That would be great!"

"You're welcome. They'll be in need of someone soon anyway."

I took Julian's hand and leaned my head against his shoulder. We walked in contented silence, passing the marina where yachts bobbed gently on the water.

"This is nice," I said, taking a deep breath of salt air.

"You seem so happy."

"I am."

"I want to take you out for dinner."

"Really? I'd love that." I hesitated. "But I can't. Exams are next week. I need to study. I've been so lazy recently, and I'm really far behind."

"So, I guess we won't be seeing each other for a while?"

"Yeah."

"And I'm leaving on the second of December, remember?"

I gulped. "I remember." I kept that fact locked in the back of my memory. I wished he hadn't brought it up again.

We passed by a small cart selling ice cream cones.

"Can I buy you an ice cream?" Julian asked.

"Of course. I can't say no to ice cream."

I chose cookies and cream, and Julian chose strawberry. We ate them as we walked towards the end of the boardwalk and then up the pier. Julian sat down, his legs dangling over the edge. I joined him. The blue water beneath us sparkled in the sunlight. I felt more relaxed than I had in a long time.

"You've got ice cream on your lip," Julian said.

Before I could lick it off, he kissed me.

36

My first exam was on Monday afternoon. Anxious students milled about the entrance to the school hall. I looked around for Lana, praying she would be there. I scanned the crowd but couldn't see her. As worry set in, I felt a tap on my shoulder.

"Looking for me?" It was Lana.

I swung around. "Thank goodness you're here."

"What? You thought I would be late again? Don't worry. I won't be collapsing halfway through either."

Lana did look much healthier and happier. She seemed back to her old self.

"Let's take a look at the seating plan," Lana said.

We made our way through the crowd to the notice board. The layout of desks was on the board, each desk with a student number assigned. I looked for my number. I would be sitting in the second row from the back.

A teacher came and herded us into a single-file line, then we made our way into the hall. I felt surprisingly calm. I sat at the desk, English exam papers in front of me. We weren't allowed to touch them until the timer started.

"You may begin," the supervisor finally announced.

Everyone opened their papers in a flurry. I read through the questions in my exam booklet, relieved I didn't find anything unexpected. The essays I had memorised would answer the questions nicely. I looked to Lana across the room, she was already zooming through the first paper. I felt relieved.

She'd be fine, and so would I. I put my pen to the page and wrote furiously for the next hour. My wrist began to strain. I managed to finish the first essay and get partway through the second one within the first hour. At just over two hours through the three-hour time limit, I had finished. I read through each essay one more time before leaving the hall. Lana had already left some time ago.

Back home, I looked over my notes for my next exam.

The process continued, day after day.

When I handed my final paper in, I felt an immense sense of relief and lightness. High school was officially over. No more exams, possibly ever.

When I got home, exhaustion hit me. All the long nights studying caught up with me at once. I fell asleep on the couch while watching television.

The next morning, I received a text message from Lana.

I have my last two exams today. Let's go out tonight to celebrate.

I typed a message back to her. *Sounds good. What exams do you have?*

Lana replied, *Scholarship bio and chem.*

So, she was doing scholarship exams as well? Lana's intelligence and work ethic never ceased to amaze me. I wished her luck. Even though she didn't need it.

When Lana's exams were finally over, we met at a local pizza restaurant. She hopped down from a bar stool and gave me a hug.

"It's over, Ivy. We've done it!"

"We have, haven't we? It feels surreal."

"In a way it's kind of sad. We'll never get to experience high school again."

"That's true. It's a weird feeling."

"I'll kind of miss it."

"Me too."

I had enjoyed my high school experience. I would miss Anna's cheery face from behind the issues desk in the library and Mr. Donaldson's infectious passion for English literature. Then there was Miss April. I would never forget her kindness when she took me to see Lana at the hospital. It had only been a day since I left, and I was already reminiscing and feeling sentimental.

"Hey, we have the rest of our lives to look forward to now. Who knows what the future will bring?" Lana said, eyes shining and a determined look on her face.

"You're right." Time to stop dwelling on the past. I had everything to look forward to now.

Lana's stomach rumbled. "I'm starving. Let's order."

We ordered cocktails and a large Margherita pizza to share.

"It's been a while since we last caught up properly," I said.

Lana nodded. "Too long. I have news."

"Me too. You first!"

"I've been accepted for two more scholarships."

"Really? That's amazing."

"One will cover my textbook costs. The other one will help with my living expenses."

"So, you're pretty much covered now?"

"Yep, just about."

Lana was absolutely killing this scholarship thing. She had worked so hard, though, I knew she deserved it.

"And you?"

My news seemed less exciting, but I told her anyway. "I've figured out what to do next year."

"Oh, yeah?"

"I'm going to work at my grandparents' lodge while concentrating on my writing in my spare time. I've decided to write a novel."

"Wow, that's so cool!"

"Yeah. I love it there, and the surroundings are so beautiful and inspiring."

"The perfect setting for an aspiring novelist."

I nodded. "Hopefully I'll be inspired to write something great."

"I knew you'd figure something out. I'll visit you when I can."

"Thanks, Lana."

The pizza arrived. I grabbed a piping-hot slice and devoured it. Lana followed suit.

"How's it going with Julian?" Lana asked when she had finished her mouthful.

"It's so wonderful. I haven't seen him for a while, though. I wanted to concentrate on my exams. But he's leaving on the second of December."

"The second? That's two days away!"

"What?"

Oh God no. I checked the date on my phone. My heart sunk.

"You're right! This is terrible. I totally lost track of the time." The thought of him leaving so soon was gut-wrenching. I felt sick to my stomach.

"You're white. Are you okay?"

No, I'm not okay. Julian was leaving, and I was completely unprepared.

"I'm just upset he's leaving so soon."

"You've known about this for a long time, Ivy."

"I must have blocked it out of my mind."

"Weren't you okay about this?"

"I thought I was. But I guess I'm not." It had been so easy not to think about it, but the reality was sinking in. Very soon, I might never see Julian again. I felt numb.

"Why don't you call him now and see what he's up to?"

Just the thought of hearing his voice again perked me up. I called him straight away. My heart beat faster with every ring, willing him to pick up. The ringing stopped.

"You have reached the mailbox of—"

I sighed, hanging up. "He's not answering."

"So, send him a message."

I typed a text message. *You're leaving soon. When can we see each other again?*

"Another piña colada, please," Lana said to the bartender. "That will make you feel better."

"Thanks."

My appetite had completely disappeared. All I could think about was Julian's impending departure. I finally understood why he had been so weary about us getting together. My feelings for him had grown stronger, and now I didn't want him to leave.

"I don't think I can do this, Lana."

"What do you mean?"

"I want more than this. I want Julian and I to be a couple."

"Oh, Ivy," Lana said, eyebrows knitted together in concern. "I think it's too late for that."

"I know. And this is what I agreed to with Julian."

The bartender placed the drink in front of me.

"I'm being silly, aren't I?" I swirled the straw in my glass.

"No, you're not. It's only natural you would feel this way."

A ringtone sounded, and I desperately scrambled for my phone.

"Uh, it's mine," Lana said.

I sipped my drink while she talked on the phone. She sounded annoyed. "What was that about?" I asked.

"It was my mum. She wants me to come home. Even though school's over, she's still really strict about how long I can stay out."

"She's just worried about you."

"I know." She sighed. "I have to go now. Mum will be outside any minute to pick me up. Do you want a ride home?"

"I'll walk."

"Will you be okay?"

I put on a brave face and nodded.

"Good. You'll get through this." She smiled reassuringly and gave me a hug before she left.

Alone at the bar, I took my time finishing my drink while deeply absorbed in my thoughts. I checked my phone periodically. Nothing.

"Would you like another drink?" the bartender asked when I had finished.

"No, thank you," I replied.

A large, loud group arrived, destroying my peace. That was my cue to leave. I walked the short distance home. When I arrived, I showered and changed into pyjamas. I stayed up for a while, listening to music to drown out my incessant thoughts. Eventually, my mind quietened down. I turned the lights off and went to bed.

I was on the cusp of drifting to sleep when my room lit up. Through bleary eyes, I searched for the light source. It was my phone screen. Suddenly alert, I reached for it. One new message from Julian.

Are you home?

Yes, I replied.

I'm coming over.

I panicked. Although I desperately wanted to see him, he couldn't come over now. I quickly messaged him back.

My parents will freak if you turn up this late.

Don't worry. Turn a light on and open your curtains.

What exactly was he planning? I did as he said, my room filling with soft lamplight. I paced anxiously. The window rattled, startling me, but it was only the wind. I curled up on my bed, phone beside me, waiting.

Finally, a new message came.

I'm here.

I went to the window. Julian stood in the garden outside my room, moonlight and shadow on his skin. He looked like a beautiful apparition, tall and heartachingly handsome. I was so relieved to see him.

He breathed on the glass and wrote "Hi" in the mist.

I opened the window. Cool night air flooded my room. "What are you doing?" I whispered.

"I had to see you," he said softly.

Not wanting to leave him standing there, I pushed the window open as far as it could go. "Come in. Don't make any noise."

Julian obliged, quietly climbing in. He stood in my room,

towering over me and eyes boring into me. I stared back, mesmerised.

"Is this a dream?" I asked.

Julian hushed me with his lips. His mouth was warm and welcoming. I pulled him closer, holding him tightly against me. We kissed deeply, completely in sync with each other. My whole body felt weak. I relented to his touch as his hands explored me. I trembled, not from nerves, but from anticipation. My thoughts were a blur, except for an overpowering desire for him.

A noise in the hallway startled us, and we broke away. I tried to catch my breath as we stood in stunned silence. The moment had passed and reason caught up with me. He couldn't stay. I didn't want to do anything I might later regret. Not to mention what would happen if we got caught.

"You better go," I whispered.

Julian nodded, understanding.

"Will I see you again?"

"Come over tomorrow."

After one last kiss on the cheek, he left out of the window, disappearing back into the night. I fell to my bed with a sigh.

37

I had never been to Julian's house before. When I pulled up outside, I double checked the address on my phone. 34 Evelyn Road.

This is it. The small townhouse's exterior was weathered, and the front garden slightly overgrown. I pressed the doorbell and waited. Finally, the door creaked open.

"Hey," Julian said. He leaned against the door frame in his white t-shirt, hair damp as if he had just gotten out of the shower. He ran a hand through it.

Seeing him caused me to flash back to our encounter the previous night. Heat rose to my cheeks. I bit my lip.

"Hey."

A hint of a smile crossed his face. He stood aside. "Come in."

Julian's luggage lined the hallway. A stark reminder he would be gone soon. I brushed the thought aside.

"I'm glad you're here. I'm all packed and ready to go. Priscilla is taking me to the airport first thing tomorrow."

He led me through the house. Its sunny yellow walls and eclectic furnishings charmed me.

"Your house is so cool."

"Thanks. It's going to be sad to leave it."

"What's going to happen to the house?"

"It's going to be put on the market. Priscilla will take care of all that. There's still a lot of packing that needs to be done."

My eyes were drawn to the pictures on the wall. Photographs of Julian's family.

"I bet you have a lot of memories here."

"Yeah."

I took a closer look at a picture of three boys, all with dark features and mischievous grins. "Is that you and your brothers?"

"Yes."

"So cute. Which one is you?"

He pointed to the boy in the middle, who was curly haired and poking his tongue out slightly.

"Adorable!"

Julian took the photo down. "I better take this. My parents will want to keep it."

We moved on to the kitchen. It had open shelves full of mismatched vintage dishes and utensils.

"There isn't much food or drink left in the fridge, but I can get you a glass of water if you want," Julian said.

"Yes, please."

He filled a glass from the tap and dropped two ice cubes in.

"Thanks." I drank it down quickly. I must have been parched.

From the dining room, a sliding door opened onto a sun-soaked veranda dotted with plants in ceramic pots. We walked outside. I leaned against the railing and looked out over the unkempt backyard. Julian stood behind me.

"About last night…" he began, a note of uncertainty in his voice.

I smiled, thinking back to that beautiful, dream-like moment in my room. "It was perfect."

"I had been out with my co-workers from Lucky Books, and I didn't see your message until I got home. I was desperate to see you."

"It was a relief to see you. I missed you so much."

"Me too." He hugged me from behind and kissed me on the head.

The sunlight dimmed as the sky filled with clouds. We went back inside just as it started to rain. I followed Julian down the hallway to a bedroom.

"Is this your room?" I asked.

"Yeah."

The large room was empty—apart from a bed, bare bookshelves, and boxes packed with all his belongings. I sat on the edge of his bed.

"So, do you know what your room in Florence will be like?"

Julian nodded. "I've seen a few photos. It's nice, but it's going to be tiny compared to this."

"You'll be spending most of your time in Barsetti's studio anyway."

"You're right." He sighed. He shuffled closer towards me and draped his arm around my back.

I leaned against his shoulder and listened to the muffled sound of his beating heart. "I wish we could stay like this."

Julian murmured in agreement. He stroked my hair, entwining his fingers in it.

I looked up at him, taking every exquisite detail in as if to try to burn his image into my brain. His dark, tousled hair, sparkling green eyes and strong jawline. I ran my hand down his chest. He let out a sigh and pulled me closer, burying his face in my hair, his arms around me. Next thing I knew, his lips were on mine. He kissed me as if his life depended on it, pressing me down onto my back, his body against mine.

All I could think about was him leaving. The cold feeling washed over me and wouldn't subside, no matter how many kisses he showered me with.

I can't do this. "Julian," I said breathlessly, pushing him away.

"What's wrong?"

I began to cry. I couldn't help it. "You're leaving," I sobbed.

Julian cradled me to his chest. "It's going to be okay."

I shook my head. "This might be the last time I see you. Ever."

"Don't say that."

"It's true."

"We'll see each other again."

"Are you sure?"

Julian nodded. "We can visit each other."

"Really?"

"You're welcome any time."

A small consolation, but I knew in my heart it wasn't enough.

"Let's just enjoy these last few moments together." He stroked my hair, calming me.

We lay side by side. I rolled over and lay my head on his warm chest. I tried my best to block out all thoughts of the future and to just enjoy this moment with him.

We spent the rest of the day in each other's arms—chatting,

laughing, kissing, and trying to keep my mind from his impending departure.

A lump formed in my throat when it was time to leave. Part of me wanted to stay longer, but I knew dragging it out wouldn't do any good. Julian walked me to the door.

"So, this is it," he said.

I didn't move. I didn't speak. He opened the door and sunlight seeped through the crack.

"Wait!" I grasped at his shirt, panicked. "I can't do this."

He stopped. The colour drained from his face.

"I don't want this."

"What do you mean?"

I couldn't keep it in any longer. The truth had to come out. "I want to be with you."

Julian stepped back, completely thrown off-guard. "You know that's not possible." His voice wavered.

"Tell me why. I don't understand."

"You'll be here. I'll be in Florence. Our lives are going in completely different directions."

"Can't we try to make it work?" I spluttered. "Plenty of people are in long-distance relationships."

Julian seemed to consider this for a moment. My heart sank when his expression settled into a pained grimace.

"It's not an option," he said solemnly.

So, this is how he truly feels… There's nothing else I can do. It took all my effort not to break down.

Julian was visibly upset. He blinked back his tears. "I'm sorry, Ivy."

I forced myself to put on a smile. "Let me know when you get there safe and sound."

"I will."

I stood on the doorstep expectantly.

"Goodbye, Ivy."

"Goodbye." I swallowed, my throat dry. *Not even an offer of a goodbye hug.*

I turned and walked back to the car, glancing over my shoulder. He stood on the doorstep, giving me a final wave goodbye. Then the door closed and it was as if I had lost him forever. I got in the car. I barely kept myself together as I drove.

So, this is what a broken heart feels like. Soon, Julian would be halfway around the world.

I didn't go straight home, instead I drove out of town until the houses became fields. Up a nearby hill, I parked at a deserted spot. I got out of the car. Standing on the edge of the hill, I screamed into the air until my voice turned hoarse. Hot tears stung my cheeks. I let it all out. A trembling, aching mess, I got back into the car and silently drove home.

Mum saw me when I opened the front door. "Are you all right?" she asked.

I opened my mouth to reply, but no words came out. Instead, I broke down into tears. "He's gone," I sobbed.

Mum didn't say anything, she just held me in her arms and led me inside.

38

I woke to the warm glow of sunlight enveloping me. I yawned and stretched, overcome by a momentary feeling of bliss. Then, everything rushed back to me, leaving a dull ache in my heart. Julian would be on the plane by now. The thought made my stomach knot. It took everything I had to drag my heavy body out of bed. I made toast for breakfast but found I didn't have the stomach for it and tossed it in the bin.

I checked my phone, yearning to see a message from Julian. Instead, I was surprised to see one from Anna.

Check out today's Flagstaff! :)

I was immediately curious and went to find the newspaper. Its usual resting place, the coffee table, was bare. I decided to ask Dad, who was sitting in front of the computer.

"Do we have today's Flagstaff?"

"Since when do you read the newspaper?" he asked, amused.

"Since now."

He smirked. "I don't have it. Ask your mother."

I found Mum sitting in the living room, cup of tea in hand.

"Do you have the newspaper?" I asked.

"I haven't read it yet."

"Please can I check something."

Hesitantly, she handed it over. My eyes were immediately drawn to a picture of Mr. Donaldson on the front page.

"That's my teacher!"

"Oh?" Mum put her reading glasses on.

I read the headline aloud. "Local teacher's secret author identity revealed." I couldn't believe it. I read the rest of the article.

High school teacher Alfred Donaldson has revealed he is author Alexander Morris. Under this name, he has ten novels published by Penguin UK. His author identity has been under wraps until his public announcement yesterday.

The news comes at the same time as his resignation from Bridgeway High School.

"I want to dedicate the rest of my years to writing," Donaldson says.

His books are often dark and disturbing.

"I want to be free from unconscious self-censorship. Even with a pen name, this was difficult as a teacher of young people."

The staff and students of Bridgeway High School will be sad to see him go.

"Alfred has been a valuable member of our staff for many years," says principal Steven Young. "It is a great loss to the English department."

"I felt it was time," says Donaldson.

Since the announcement, Penguin have expressed interest in distributing his titles in Australasia.

"Mr. Donaldson is leaving Bridgeway High," I said,

surprisingly upset. I wondered whether my talk with him had influenced his decision. I hadn't meant for him to leave his job.

"You're not going back to school anyway," Mum reminded me. She took the newspaper from me and read the article. "To think your English teacher is a successful author..."

"Didn't I tell you that?"

Mum scratched her head. "Hmmmm... That's right. You did. I'm sorry I didn't take it more seriously."

"That's okay."

"Mr. Donaldson encouraged you with your writing, didn't he?"

I nodded.

Mum smiled. "He must have seen potential in you."

"Yes, I think so."

"Maybe this writing thing will work out for you after all."

Her gentle admission meant the world to me. "Thanks, Mum. I really hope so." I couldn't linger on her words for long.

A sharp and urgent knock at the door made me jump. "Are we expecting someone?"

Mum's brow furrowed in confusion. "I don't think so." She put down her cup of tea and started to get up.

"Don't worry. I'll get it."

"Thanks." She sat back down. "If it's someone trying to sell something, tell them we're not interested."

I answered the door. Julian stood there, messy-haired, red-eyed. I gaped at him, too shocked to speak.

He shuffled nervously on his feet. "Ivy..."

"What happened?" I spluttered. "Aren't you supposed to be on a plane right now?"

"There's been a turn of events. My flight has been delayed. I don't have much time."

"Why are you here?"

"I couldn't leave things the way they were."

I was deeply aware that our conversation could be overheard. "Let's go somewhere and talk." I led Julian to the garden behind the house. In the cover of trees, we continued our conversation.

"What happened?" I asked, studying his face for clues. He looked as though he had aged about five years overnight.

Slowly, he chose his words. "I kept thinking about what you said about us. About the possibility of staying together..."

The painful memory was still fresh in my mind. "You shot that down pretty quick."

Julian looked down, ashamed. "I thought turning you down was the right thing to do. It would set you free to live your life."

"But I want *you* in my life," I pleaded.

"I know, and I felt terrible. I couldn't sleep last night, thinking about what I'd done. Deep down, I knew the truth, and I couldn't deny it any longer."

My heart pounded on overdrive, and my body was so tense I could snap. *What is he going to say?*

"Ivy," Julian stepped towards me. He took my hand in his. "I don't want this to be the end of us. I want it to be the beginning."

I cried. I couldn't help it. So much emotion had been pent up inside me, and now, it poured out freely.

Julian frowned, concern in his eyes. "What's wrong? Have I upset you?"

I shook my head, wiping away my tears. "I'm just so happy."

"So, you'll be my girlfriend, then?"

"Yes. Of course, I will!"

"Then let's make a promise."

"What promise?"

"To reunite. When I have finished my first year of studies. When you have finished writing your novel. Meet me in Florence. I want you to come."

He didn't need to elaborate. Of course, the answer was yes.

"I will."

Julian flung his arms around me. "I can't wait." He squeezed me so tight he lifted me up off the ground.

"Me too." Wrapped up in his arms, I felt overjoyed. I kissed him on the lips.

We were unable to contain our grins.

He broke away. "I'm sorry. I have to go now. My flight will be leaving soon."

I nodded. Nothing would ruin my happiness now, not even him having to leave.

He was about to go, but he hesitated. "Ivy?"

"Yes?"

"I love you."

Fresh tears rolled down my cheeks. "I love you, too."

39

Three months later

On a blazing summer day, a gentle breeze rustled through the lush green trees surrounding me. Cicadas chirped and water trickled in a nearby stream. Warm sunlight caressed my skin. I smiled, full of peace. I approached the structure ahead of me.

What was once an old, rundown shed had been transformed into a beautiful log cabin. This was my new home. I held the key tight in my hand. When I reached the door, I noticed a package waiting on the doorstep. I stooped down and picked it up. Turning it over in my hands, I saw it was from Julian. The return address was Flat 12C, Via Velenze, Altrarno, Florence.

My heart pounded. I took the package inside. My suitcase was on the bed since I still hadn't unpacked. I heaved it off and sat down with the package on my knees. When I tore it open, an envelope and a gift-wrapped present fell out. I opened the envelope first. Inside was a letter. I unfolded it and read.

Dear Ivy,

It's half past seven in the morning. From my apartment window, I can see the sun rising over the Arno river. It has been a month since I moved to Florence. I enjoyed spending time with my parents in France, but it is good to finally get settled here.

Italian lessons have been consuming my days. I still don't feel prepared. My classes with Alberto Barsetti begin in two weeks. I'm anxious and excited.

Florence is just beautiful. You would love it here. Every street is brimming with little art studios and galleries, bakeries, cafés and gelato vendors.

It's an art-lover's paradise here. You're surrounded by so much art that it's overwhelming. I have already visited so many galleries that I think I've overdone it. The art here is to be enjoyed slowly—savoured. I have to keep reminding myself I'm going to be here for a long time. There's no point in rushing.

I'm living with an Italian guy, Gio. He's a little older than me and a graphic designer. It's great living with a local. He knows all the best spots around town.

Living here still feels so surreal, but I know with time, this is going to feel like home.

How are you, Ivy? I think about you every day. I can't help it. We had something good going on. It's just the timing was all wrong. I'm counting down the days until we see each other again.

I hope you enjoy your gift. It's from a little bindery where they sell hand-crafted stationery. You would love it.

Please write back to me. I might not always be able to reply straight away, but trust me, I will keep in touch. It's going to be a challenging life ahead of me. I know you will be working hard too.

Don't give up on your writing.

Love,

Julian

Tears welled up in my eyes as I read. I had been doing my best to stay strong since Julian's departure, but the letter brought my feelings surging back in full force. I was so overjoyed to hear from him. The gift, wrapped in exquisitely patterned paper, was heavy on my lap. I opened it, peeling away layers of paper to reveal a thick leather journal. I ran my fingers over the cover, supple and smooth. I opened the book to feel the soft and creamy pages, waiting to be filled up with words.

I will write in this notebook every day. I promise.

...

Made in the USA
Middletown, DE
05 January 2020

82596236R00163